W9-ANQ-601

The Year We Missed My Birthday

eleven birthday stories

Edited by Lois Metzger

Scholastic Inc.

New York   Toronto   London   Auckland   Sydney
Mexico City   New Delhi   Hong Kong   Buenos Aires

"The Secret" © 2005 by Lois Lowry
"One Wing" © 2005 by Ann Cameron
"Not a Piñata This Year" © 2005 by Alma Flor Ada
"The Year We Missed My Birthday" © 2005 by Amy Goldman Koss
"Celebration" © 2005 by Nora Raleigh Baskin
"Happy Birthday to Hugh" © 2005 by Lois Metzger
"With Love, From Mom and Dad" © 2005 by Rita Williams-Garcia
"Sez You" © 2005 by Norma Fox Mazer
"Opposite of Miffy" © 2005 by Lisa Yee
"The Girl in the Mirror" © 2005 by Cynthia D. Grant
"Oh Happy Day!" © 2005 by Sharon Robinson

ISBN 0-439-73563-7

Copyright © 2005 by Lois Metzger

12 11 10 9 8 7 6 5 4 3 2 1   5 6 7 8 9 10/0

Printed in the U.S.A.

First printing, October 2005

Contents

Foreword

Some holidays celebrate countries or famous people or mothers or fathers or religions or family gatherings. But there's only one holiday that celebrates *you*—and that's your birthday.

In a way, a birthday is like a scorecard, counting up the years since you arrived on the planet. In another way, it's a step on a journey—especially during the middle years, as childhood gets left behind and you're facing all the mysteries that lie ahead.

Sometimes the path looks clear, bright, filled with light, and you can see far into the distance. Sometimes it's much foggier.

A birthday gets you wondering about these things.

You are invited . . .

Here are eleven birthday presents from eleven writers who have written new stories just for this book. They've written about characters whose hopes were high, whose hopes were dashed, whose greatest wishes come true, and who get more than they could possibly have imagined.

Lois Lowry's story takes place in a world where birthdays aren't celebrated at all, but the sheer joy of a birthday creates its own celebration. In Cynthia Grant's story, a girl's best friends have forgotten her birthday. In Amy Goldman Koss's story, a girl's best friends *steal* her birthday. Ann Cameron has written about a girl who insists on perfection, particularly on her birthday—and finds that a day that's far from perfect can still be amazing.

In every story, thinking about birthdays helps people discover more about who they are, who they've been, and who they are becoming.

Here's wishing you happiness on your birthdays and on all the days in between.

—Lois Metzger

The Secret

by Lois Lowry

Perhaps it was a long time ago. Perhaps it is a time yet to come. Or might it possibly be now, in a place we cannot name?

A baby is born. A small boy, with wisps of hair that grow into curls as the months pass, and with eyes that are often wide with curiosity or crinkled with merriment: eyes that, when the little one sleeps, are fringed with lashes against his cheek as if a fragile spiderweb had been constructed there.

His parents, who had longed for this child, who had celebrated his birth, watch with joy as the months pass, as their little one smiles for the first time, then one day laughs aloud as if the world is a place designed for his enjoyment. They smile with pride when he sits, wobbles, and reaches for a toy with his chubby hands. They coax him with tidbits of food and they notice with pride when his first small teeth appear, and listen with delight when he tries to form sounds that have meaning.

But they experience all of this—the celebrating, the glee, the delight—privately. Secretly. It is not that babies are forbidden in this place. Not at all. Everyone gives birth and so the human species continues. When this couple takes their small boy with them on their excursions, they greet others who have little ones, nodding politely. But only in secret, guiltily, do they confide in each other:

Our boy is handsomer than any other.

Did you get a look at that baby at the park? It didn't seem as sturdy as ours.

Have you noticed how intelligent he is? Much more than any other his age.

These thoughts are whispered behind closed doors, only to each other, for this is a place where pride is considered a sin. Delight is forbidden. Joy is obsolete. Love does not exist.

They know this, though they do not know the words for pride or delight or joy, for those words have disappeared into the past, and no longer have usage or meaning. Many such words exist on a list that forbids them, a list the people no longer bother to consult.

The couple knows that they are not allowed to rejoice.

And they are obedient, law-abiding people.

But even without knowing the word for what they feel, they cannot keep themselves from loving this beautiful child.

One day, carefully, he plants one tiny foot parallel to the other, appears to think about this, and then lifts himself and takes a step. Then another. With the third step he wobbles, falls, whimpers, and then tries again.

The couple, his parents, clap their hands as he walks for the first time.

It is true, they know, that every human has done this. Yet as they watch this child, it appears miraculous and wonderful. *Look!* They say to each other. *Look at him!* And it is hard for them to conceal their smiles.

There are new leaves on the trees on that day that he walks, and some small purple flowers have just bloomed. It is not a colorful place, the place where these people live, for the sky is always coated with thin clouds and the air itself seems gray. But flowers do force themselves up in the dim light, and on the day that the child takes his first steps, some have just opened.

The mother of the child counts back in her mind,

through the months. "There were purple flowers on the day he was born," she tells the father of the child, who nods and remembers it. "Grape hyacinths."

"And tulips in bloom when he smiled. It was two months later," the father recalled.

"It was fall when he sat up alone for the first time. The leaves were turning color."

"Yes, and winter, when we noticed the teeth. The tiny white teeth, and the snow was the same white."

"Now he walks. And the little purple flowers, the grape hyacinths, are in bloom again! It is a year since the day he was born."

They decide it is an event to commemorate. Their child has been on this earth for a year.

They pull the curtains closed. Not that anyone would prowl about and peer through their windows. At least they don't think that would happen. But it is better to be careful, and private.

The woman, the child's mother, bakes a small cake, using flour and eggs and sugar and milk: a delicate cake crusted golden when she takes it from the oven. The little boy, still wobbling on his chubby legs, reaches toward it with excitement, but they laugh and say gently, "Wait. It must cool first."

She spreads a tablecloth over their table, and ties a ribbon into a large bow on the back of the child's high chair, not even knowing why, but feeling that something must single him out, on this day. Then the woman says to her husband, "We should do this every year. We should—what is the word?"

He thinks. "Celebrate," he says. And he agrees with her. "Yes, we should. Every year."

"Is that on the list?" his wife asks anxiously as she lifts the small boy into his chair.

"No. I'm sure it isn't. We celebrate the elections. They use the word. We all do."

It is true. When the government changes, as it does periodically, a band plays, marching down the avenues, and it is designated a celebration. People are allowed to say the word.

This is not exclusively a small-town event, though the couple and their child live in a small town. The change of government is an event that all small and large towns, and cities vast and far away, celebrate. The celebration spans across oceans and deserts; multitudes of people watch and applaud as governmental bands and regiments march under the gray, grim skies in cities and towns throughout the earth.

The woman touches the cake lightly and determines that it is cool enough. "It's your birth day," she says to the small boy, and she ties a bib around his neck.

"Can you say that? Birth day?" she asks him, but he is still only one year new, and has not yet mastered the making of sounds. He grins, and reaches toward the cake.

"Wait!" his father says suddenly. He takes a small candle from a drawer, presses it into the center of the cake, and lights it. The baby watches the small flame intently, his eyes wide. The man and woman, holding hands, watch their child.

Then they blow out the flame and feed him a small piece of the sweet cake.

The curtains are closed against the world and they believe they are the only ones. But far away, across a wide river, in a distant city, another couple lights a candle that has been placed on a cake, and watch their little girl, who has also been on the earth for just a year, as she claps her hands in delight.

There are others as well. Some the day before, too. And the day before that.

The months pass, and the purple flowers die back to make way for the later spring blossoms, and then the tulips and daffodils wilt under the gray skies, and hardier summer flowers take their place. The small boy not only walks now, but runs on his sturdy legs, and his parents, laughing, chase him to keep him safe from danger.

He begins to form words, and points, and asks for things.

The parents do their daily work, the jobs they are

required to do, and they fulfill all their obligations. They obey the laws and follow the rules. If you see them walking in the town, they seem ordinary, even dull, moving about on their errands, pushing their child in his little wheeled cart, nodding to acquaintances. Even the child appears dull, his eyes a bit vacant, his demeanor listless.

But in their home, in secret, they disobey. It is like an illness, their ferocious love for their son, which makes them hug and laugh and play. They chase him and he runs, squealing with pleasure. They throw a small ball back and forth. They tickle him until he shrieks with laughter.

By the time the leaves begin to fall, in autumn, he can say a few words. He calls them *Mama* and *Papa* and he asks for things now, instead of pointing. He asks for milk, and water, and toys, using the names, forming the words for "chair" and "hot" and even "no," which he sometimes says with a pout, shaking his head back and forth, making them chuckle.

He tastes snowflakes with surprise, when they fall in winter. They show him glistening icicles hanging from tree branches one morning after a storm. The mother makes mittens for his small hands: red mittens, and she begins to teach him the words for colors. *No other child his age knows colors*, the woman says to her husband, when the boy has told them blue, and green, and yellow correctly. *He is the smartest child anywhere.*

"Shhhh," the child's father replies, for they are outside. He reaches down and pats the boy's shoulder in approval but only after he has looked around to be certain he is not observed.

"Sorry," his wife replies, for in her excitement for the boy's achievements she has forgotten that pride must be hidden.

When the snow melts, small purple flowers begin to spring up from the earth.

"Two!" the woman realizes. "He has been with us now for two years." She goes to the cupboard for the ingredients and begins to make a cake.

This time, at the celebration, the little boy can say the words. "Birth day!" he says in his high, clear voice, when they tell him the name of the occasion.

"Light!" he says, in awe, when they light two candles on the cake. Then they show him how, and they watch, smiling, as he manages to blow out the two small candles, first one, then the other.

Again, they have drawn the curtains. They have been so careful. No one knows how much they love the child.

And they do not know that they are not alone. In a small house perched against the side of a high mountain on the other side of the world, behind closed shutters, a family watches their child blow out four candles.

In a hot place, in an open hut where chickens peck at the dry dirt floor, a child blows out seven candles and grins.

It happens the next day, and the next, and the ones after that. Not to the little boy, for his birth day has passed now. But each day is a birth day for someone who is loved. Separately, the secret celebrations take place.

The purple flowers disappear and the summer blossoms come and go. Leaves fall. Snow comes. The boy grows.

Then it is time once again. There are three candles now for the beloved child, and surprisingly (*he is brilliant, no question*, the mother whispers to her husband) the boy remembers what the occasion is. "Birth day," he announces, when the cake comes out of the oven, fragrant and moist. "Birthday," he says again, slurring the two words, making them one.

He blows out the three candles on his first try. His parents clap and watch the tiny wisps of smoke rise from the extinguished wax. But surprisingly, the boy does not reach for the sweet cake as he has in the previous years. He seems—odd for a child so small—lost in thought. He tilts his head and closes his eyes, as if trying to remember something.

Then he looks at them and says a word.

The woman is confused. It is not a word she has heard before. She looks to her husband.

The boy's father is startled at first, then frightened. "It's forbidden," he whispers. "I'm almost certain. Get the list."

His wife rummages on the shelf. They have not looked at it in years. There has been no need. Finally she finds the printed list tucked inside a reference book. She gives it to her husband, and he unfolds it and turns the pages, moving his finger down the alphabetized lines. A, B, C, D, E, F, G, H. He stops at H.

"Yes, here it is," he says. "It's forbidden. I barely remember it. I've never heard it said. How did he—"

They watch, too astonished to grab and restrain him, as their small son climbs from his chair, goes to the window, and draws the curtain open. It is a spring morning and the window is raised to the open air. The tiny purple blossoms of grape hyacinth carpet the lawn. They have bloomed there every year at this time. But today, the birth day, they look different.

There is sunshine on them. A sliver has opened in the gray smear of sky, and a ray of sun has cut its way through and cast a golden light on the flowers.

They cannot hold back their boy. Perhaps the truth

of it is that they do not want to. They simply watch, and listen, as he leans from the window into the sunlight and calls the forbidden word aloud in his clear child's voice.

"Happy!" he calls out. "Happy birthday!"

Then they begin to hear it echoed. From other houses, from other towns, from cities far away, across wide rivers and beyond mountains, the clear voices of beloved children too young to know, the quavering voices of ancient ones too old to fear, and of countless others too brave to care about the danger of it, comes a chorus of the forbidden word, the punishable phrase. The strength and timbre of the thousands of voices shake the earth itself.

"Happy Birthday!"

Other words break loose then, and they all are spoken aloud, and shouted, and sung, into the golden light of change.

Perhaps this happened once? Perhaps it will one day? Perhaps it is happening someplace right now.

One Wing

by Ann Cameron

A person's birthday is the most special day of the year. On your birthday, everybody should show they know how special you really are and give you the respect you deserve. Even if, on other days, they forget, on your birthday they're not supposed to.

They're not supposed to—but still, they might. So I was careful. I planned my birthday party so everybody would treat me right and everything would come out perfect.

I was going to be ten. For the first time, it would take two numbers to write my age. I felt old and ready to understand everything—like someone who has climbed a high mountain almost to the top and is about to see the whole world for the first time.

My mom had just gotten a raise at her job, so she

14

didn't say no, a party would be too expensive. She even looked happy about the idea. She said, "Sure, Peregrine—plan it just how you want."

As you now know, my name is Peregrine. My mom named me that because, when she was pregnant with me, she came across that word in a book on birds.

"Peregrine" means "pilgrim." It's also the name of a special falcon—one that makes long journeys and is the fastest-flying bird on earth.

My mother says that when she saw that word for the first time and pronounced it aloud to herself, she thought it was the most beautiful word she had ever heard.

It's nice, that she wanted to name me for the most beautiful word she ever heard. Sometimes I say it to myself and I can hear the beauty of it and feel a shining powerful spirit in it, soaring on the wind.

Other times, though, I feel the opposite. I think if it hadn't been for Mom's coming across that word, maybe she'd have thought of a more everyday name for me, like "Pat" or "Pam," and then I would've been like everybody else. And I would've felt normal, one hundred percent of the time. Whatever being normal feels like. I'm not sure, except that, if you're named Pat or Pam, your name slides into a conversation easy, like it belongs there, so you probably always feel like you fit in. If you're named Peregrine, sometimes you wonder.

I wanted to invite just friends to the party, but for a birthday when you're ten, you can't—mostly I guess because when you're ten you're old enough to owe people favors or want them to owe you favors.

I did invite my best friend, Ariel, and my neighbor, Lindsay. Lindsay is my age and we play together a lot. But I had to invite Lindsay's sister, Tiffany, too. Tiffany is younger than Lindsay and acts like a baby, but their mom would have been mad if I didn't invite her.

Megan, I used to fight with. She once kidnapped my doll and hid it under a bush, but she's a neighbor so I invited her because she also would have been mad otherwise.

I invited Samantha, who's in my class, because we both like turtles.

I invited Susan. I don't like Susan a whole lot, but she'd invited me to her birthday party, so I had to invite her to mine. It's almost like a law that you have to do this. No matter how boring the birthday party was that you went to, you have to invite the person who gave it to yours.

I invited Maria, even though she isn't a friend. She's really popular, in fact she's the most popular girl in my class, and I thought if she came to my party, maybe she'd become my friend and then I'd get to be popular like her. Not that anybody hates me. It's not that bad.

I invited Lauren. I don't really like Lauren much AT ALL, but I invited her because of the present I would get.

Every time a girl has a birthday party and Lauren is invited, Lauren's dad, who is a professional artist, paints a special wooden treasure box with a unique, individual painting just for the birthday girl. I told Lauren I wanted her dad to paint a cocker spaniel on my treasure box and she promised he would do it.

I wanted a cocker spaniel painted on my box because in real life I would like to have a real one, but I can't have a dog because of my allergies.

That's not quite true. Maybe I could have a naked dog, with no fur. My mom says there is such a breed, and we could get one, but who wants a dog with no fur? I don't. A dog with no fur would be very far from perfect.

I asked Lauren to ask her dad if he could please paint the dog on the treasure box so you could see some individual hairs. That way, no one would ever mistake it for a naked dog.

I didn't invite Eugene to my party. He lives right next door, but I didn't ask him because if he knew he was the only boy invited, he wouldn't come. Or, if he did come, he'd be embarrassed and everybody would say I had a boyfriend, and never quit saying it for weeks or months. Maybe even years. I didn't even tell him I was having a party.

It was going to be a Crazy Outfit party, where whoever was dressed the craziest would win a prize. I thought that would be fun, and everybody I invited liked that idea, too. Maybe they thought they could win. But I already had a plan for the craziest possible outfit and I was sure I'd be the best.

The day of the party came, January 4th. When the living room was all decorated, I fastened some crepe paper and some extra balloons to a bush in our yard. Eugene came out then, but when he saw me tying up balloons, he turned around and went home without even saying, "Happy birthday!" However, he is a boy and that is how boys act, so I didn't care.

When it came time for the party to start, I couldn't go to the door because of my costume, so my mom did. Everybody crowded in at once, in front of Lauren's and Samantha's mothers, who had driven some kids over.

They were all dressed special. Over her regular clothes, Ariel was wearing her ice skates with the guards on, and carrying a broom. Lindsay had on a tie-dyed T-shirt, raggedy cutoffs, and swim fins on her feet. Her little sister, Tiffany, was dressed as a pink bunny rabbit. Megan had on a man's tie with palm trees painted on it, and a very tall pointed black hat. Samantha had on a cardboard turtle-shell costume. Susan was wearing yellow pants, a yellow shirt, and yellow shoes, with sparkles sprinkled all over the whole outfit that were coming off on the rug. Maria wore two different masks, a ghost mask facing front, and a famous TV anchorwoman mask facing backward, so she looked like two different people. Lauren had on huge rubber boots and carried an umbrella.

Ariel was the first one to see me in the corner of the living room. She screamed and pointed and dropped her broom. Then everybody screamed. Maria lowered her ghost mask and smiled her beautiful popular-girl smile. "Awesome!" she said, and I hoped that meant she'd want me to be a close friend.

Tiffany hopped up and I think she would have hugged me, except she couldn't get that close. Nobody could. My needles stuck out all over.

I was a Christmas tree.

My base layer was green pajama bottoms and a green sweatshirt with a hood. Over that, I was covered in plastic pine branches, with silver, red, and gold Christmas ornaments hooked on. On top of my hood, a velvet Santa Claus was sitting on a cascade of silver tinsel that fell down in front of my eyes. All the Christmas lights we'd had on our tree were wound around my body, and I was plugged in, blinking on and off, on and off.

I looked stupendous.

We played some games where I didn't have to move very much—throwing games with beanbags and then a charade guessing game. I wasn't very good at throwing because I couldn't move my arms much, so I didn't win at that. Tiffany won a chocolate bar, which she ate immediately, and since she was little, nobody said she couldn't, but she was supposed to have taken it home.

Then it was Crazy Outfit judging time. Samantha's mom took pictures of all of us. The three mothers—Samantha's, Lauren's, and mine—asked everybody to walk around in a circle while they decided who was best.

Everybody but me held hands and walked around in a circle in the living room. I couldn't, because I was plugged in. But that didn't matter—the mothers weren't going to leave me out.

They got in their own little circle across the room and whispered to each other. We waited, everybody patting her own costume one more time, trying to make sure it looked perfect.

The huddle of the moms broke up. Samantha's

mom looked us up and down. "The winner is—" she began.

I waited to hear my name.

"—Maria!"

I couldn't believe it! Maria's outfit wasn't original! It was just masks from a store!

My outfit was the best, and all the moms had to know it!

My very own mother—who had to know better!!!—gave Maria the prize, a troll doll.

"Let's applaud Maria now!" Samantha's mom said.

Everybody applauded. Not me. I couldn't applaud with my arms tied to pine branches. Also, I didn't want to.

I stared at Maria through my cascade of silver tinsel. I waited for her to refuse the troll doll because she didn't deserve it, and tell the mothers and everybody else that she was proud to be doing the right thing on my birthday and giving the troll doll to me.

She definitely didn't do the right thing, though. No, she just raised her ghost mask and smiled her beautiful popular-girl smile and said, "Thank you!" Like she had really won. Like she really deserved that troll doll, which was a jewel troll doll, too, with a purple jewel for its belly button.

My mom smiled at Maria and at the same time

darted her eyes toward me. I could feel them boring right through all my silver tinsel, telling me without a word that I had better change my face and smile, that I had better not complain, and I had better be nice.

It was as if she was enforcing the law of birthdays that, no matter how miserable they are, you have to pretend they are fun.

The only good thing after that was the pizza. Also, when the pizza deliveryman caught a glimpse of me, he said, "Holy Moly!" He should have been the judge, not the moms.

The moms arranged chairs and little tables around the living room so we could eat. I was going to sit down, but I couldn't because of my lights. My mom whispered to me that it would be all right to unplug, but I said I would *not* unplug, so she went over to Eugene's house to borrow an extension cord.

Lauren's and Samantha's mothers brought in paper plates, and passed the pizza around. My mom attached the extension cord from Eugene's house into my string of lights. They were only out for a split second at the very most.

I moved some of the lights higher so I wouldn't be sitting on them, and lost one pine branch from one arm. It didn't matter so much anymore, though, and without that one branch, I could eat.

My mom brought in the giant square ice-cream cake with the frosting design I had specially picked out—the one with the girl talking on a pink cell phone. Everybody sang,

Happy birthday, dear Peregrine!

"Peregrine! She's a pretty nice person for a tree," Lauren said, and all the girls, even my best friend, Ariel, laughed, and Lauren started singing,

CHRIS-mas Tree, O CHRIS-mas Tree
how bright thy LIGHTS are SHI-ning!

Much later I thought maybe she was complimenting me, but at the time I knew she was insulting me. And she would have gotten everybody to sing it, but Susan told her to stop, so she did.

Which is a good thing, because I don't know what I would have done if she had kept it up.

Lauren likes to make fun of people. That's why I don't like her AT ALL.

"Make a wish!" my mother said. She didn't even notice that I had been insulted on my birthday.

I looked down at all the sweet little pink candles on the cell-phone-theme cake and wished my party was over. Then I got scared by my own bad wish and added on an extra, that something good would still happen on my birthday.

I blew out all the candles with one breath. I cut the cake. I really wanted the piece with the pink cell phone, because it looked like it was made of thick strawberry-cream icing, but Ariel took that slice while I was still cutting the rest. I never even got to taste it.

Everybody gave me presents—mostly the kind you expect. Susan's present was the most boring—socks, just plain, regular white socks with no designs. The best was from Lauren, of course—the treasure box with a cocker spaniel painted on it. It was better than any of the ones Lauren's father had ever painted. The cocker spaniel was in different positions on all four sides of the box and the top. His eyes were shining with dog love, and you could see for sure that he had wavy hair and lots of it.

I only wished he hadn't come from Lauren.

That was pretty much the end of the party. Lauren put her rubber boots back on; she had taken them off after they got very hot. Ariel, whose ankles had hurt her, put her ice skates back on. Maria thanked the moms for her prize and they said she deserved it. Everybody thanked everybody for everything and said they had a nice time. Everybody said good-bye. The front door closed, shutting out them and the cold.

"Now!" my mother said. She unplugged me and took off all my ornaments, all my lights and the pine branches. I was very itchy, and I scratched my legs through my green pajamas.

"Mom! I should have WON!" I said. "You know I should have!"

"Nobody wins the main party prize on her birthday," my mom said calmly. Like it was the law or something.

"But the person who is the best should win!"

My mom sighed. "At a birthday, if it's your party, it'll never happen."

"Why not?" I yanked on tinsel that had crawled down the neck of my green sweatshirt.

"Because, the birthday person gets all the attention, and all the presents the guests bring, and it wouldn't be fair if the birthday person ALSO hogs the main party prize, too."

It was a law. A law of life. I scratched under my green sweatshirt and tried to accept it.

"Why didn't you tell me that beforehand?"

"You wouldn't have listened," my mom said. "Or, if you had listened, it would've spoiled everything for you."

"I wanted my birthday to be perfect!" I said. "I planned it all out! I made every last thing right!"

"Peregrine," my mom said. "Nobody can make perfection. It flashes by sometimes. The best you can do is keep an eye out for it. Throw it a kiss. Then, just for an instant, you are part of it."

My eyes felt red. My nose felt itchy. Something from my costume was starting up my allergies.

"You don't believe me, do you?" my mom said.

I shook my head. "Whatever goes away right away, that's not perfection!"

I wanted to cry. I had cried on every birthday I'd ever had in my whole life, but I didn't this time, because I was ten and too old for that.

My mom hugged me and rubbed my back. She stroked my hair and got more tinsel out of it. She told me I was beautiful. She didn't make the mistake of wishing me a happy birthday.

"Why don't you put on your regular clothes and go see Eugene? He's probably been feeling very left out."

I hadn't thought of that.

I took the treasure box to show him. He got a big smile on his face when he saw me at the door. We sat down in his living room.

"I got this from Lauren," I said.

"It's cool." Eugene turned the treasure box all around, looking at each and every dog.

"Lauren's dad painted it. But you know what? I almost don't want it. Lauren made fun of me at my party."

"Lauren always tries to get attention by making jokes," Eugene said. "Maybe she just meant to be funny."

"She wasn't."

"Well, so, probably nobody really thought she was funny, either. If they laughed, they were just being polite."

"Maybe."

Eugene opened the treasure box. It was empty, of course, but it opened perfectly on its little golden hinges.

"Just enjoy the box and forget the bad part. That's what I would do," Eugene said. "I watched your party from our bathroom window. I saw the games and everything. I guess it must have been a Crazy Outfit party. Yours was the best."

"The prize was a troll doll. But I didn't win."

"Yours was the best, though," Eugene said. "You had the craziest idea. Everybody really liked it, I bet."

"Maybe," I said. Eugene is the kind of friend who can always make you feel better. That's one reason I have always liked him.

He set the treasure box down.

"I made you something for your birthday, too. But it didn't come out quite right. Should I show you? You probably won't want it."

"Show me," I said.

"Close your eyes, then, and hold out your hands."

I felt something heavy and odd-shaped. I opened my eyes. I was holding a wooden angel, softly rounded and sanded smooth. Eugene told me he had carved it for me.

It wore a flowing robe. It had one wide feathery wing, half opened.

"It was perfect until my knife slipped," Eugene said, "that's when I cut the other wing off. So, if you don't want it, you don't have to keep it."

I stood it up on the palm of my hand. It had a good expression on its brown face, calm and beautiful—as if it didn't mind having only one wing.

"I like it," I said. "Thank you, Eugene. I like it a lot."

Not a Piñata This Year

by Alma Flor Ada

"Please, Mother. I want a birthday party, not a Cinco de Mayo celebration." Juanita wasn't drinking her hot chocolate. She hadn't even touched her pan dulce, the pastry she loved so much.

"But, Juanita, what do you mean? Piñatas are for birthdays, too."

"Not in this country! I want a *regular* birthday."

"Juanita, I only want you and your friends to have a good time. What does *regular* mean?" There was no question her mother sincerely wanted to understand her.

Juanita sighed deeply and answered with undisguised impatience, "It means we buy everything at Toy World and nothing at the stores in the barrio where you always shop. We don't have a piñata, we don't hang papel picado, and we don't play any games like el plato or las latas."

Miguel couldn't stay silent anymore. He finished his hot chocolate in one last gulp. "We had a lot of fun playing el plato during your last birthday party!" he told his sister.

"Miguel, stay out of this, please. Last year we had family friends at my birthday party. This year I'm inviting my school friends!"

"Don't worry, Juanita. I'll make the party just as you want it—now don't be late for school."

Juanita smiled for the first time all morning.

"Thanks, Mom. I knew you would understand. We're in this country now so we should be like everyone else. My birthday is going to be like the ones I have read about in so many books!"

Juanita picked up her backpack. She was almost at the door when she returned and gave her mother a quick kiss. "And remember, Mom, we don't need food. There won't be any adults here. And don't bake me a cake. I want a cake from Safeway."

Miguel looked at the pained expression on his mother's face and rushed to give her a hug. Her mother always had so much fun decorating cakes for them. They didn't look store-bought, but they were festive and inventive and, on top of that, delicious.

"Don't worry, Mami. She'll outgrow this."

When his mother looked at him surprisedly, Miguel added, "She'll be different when she turns twenty-one."

His mother could only laugh. Miguel was barely ten and Juanita was going to be eleven, but he certainly sounded like the older child.

"Everyone does not need to be as alike as Juanita thinks to have fun," she told her son as she stroked his hair. "Look at us. Your birthday parties have always been a mixture of things I love from your father's Mexican background, and the traditional games of my Cuban family. I'm sure our parties have never been like anyone else's but, the truth is, everyone has enjoyed them."

Miguel gave her a sunny smile and left for school.

Her birthday morning seemed brighter than any other, and Juanita jumped easily out of bed. She did her stretches and had almost finished getting dressed when her mother walked proudly into her room, holding a party dress in her arms.

Juanita frowned but, not wanting to hurt her mother, she said, "It's very pretty, Mom. I'll wear it to Berta's wedding next week."

Obviously, that had not been her mother's intention for the dress, but all she said was, "Feliz cumpleaños, cariño. I hope your day is all you expect!"

After her mother left, Juanita hung the dress in her closet. She was not going to wear all that frill and lace to her birthday party. She would look really cool in the powder-blue top and the faded blue jeans she had convinced her mother to buy for her.

Once she finished dressing, she looked at herself in the mirror. She shook her head, still experiencing a new sense of freedom. Her head felt light since there was no long hair trailing along with her movements. Convincing her mother to let her get rid of her long hair had taken some doing. Some part of her missed the thick smooth hair that had hung in braids all her life. But here she was, a whole new Juanita, ready for a whole new year of her life.

Juanita and Miguel set the table with the paper tablecloth, and paper plates and cups, and they put out the shiny party hats. Then they set out a tray of plastic toys in party-favor bags.

Miguel remembered Juanita's birthday party last year, the table covered with an embroidered tablecloth and set with their best dishes. The walls had been decked with strings of papel picado, showing the clever designs made by folding and cutting the silk paper. Miguel felt different, and he wondered if Juanita would feel the difference as he did. There was not much time for comparisons, though, because the guests were just arriving.

Juanita stood at the door in her jeans, greeting the twelve girls she had invited to her party. To her surprise, some of the parents came into the house with their daughters. She had not expected that. Weren't American parents supposed to just leave their kids at the door and come back for them at the end of the party? She had carefully written on the invitations that the time of the party was from 3:00 to 6:00 PM. But, of course, all she could do now as people approached was smile at everyone.

Her classmates' outfits were also quite a surprise. Yes, Jessica and Camille were wearing jeans, and Emma had on a cute jumpsuit, but Mikaela was wearing a sari, Janice had on a Chinese silk jacket over silk black pants, Samantha was wearing an elaborate, violet velvet dress, and Victoria was wearing a tutu over her leotards. "I've come right from ballet lessons—I hope you don't mind," she had said to Juanita's mother, making a bow like a ballerina. Lori, Cristina, and Jennifer all wore different colored dresses.

Several of the mothers walked in with covered dishes that filled the house with surprising and enticing smells.

None of it looked much like the birthday party

she had imagined, but Juanita was excitedly placing gifts on the side table.

The girls had all been talking and giggling in small groups for a while when Juanita approached her mother. "Mom, can you help us get started with the pin-the-tail-on-the-donkey game?"

When Juanita's mother called the girls to the wall where the donkey poster was taped, Lori said, "Do we really need to play that game? We have been playing that for years. Someone said you knew different games."

"Where's the piñata?" asked Jennifer.

"We're not having a piñata! Why did you think we would have one?" Juanita's voice sounded a little hurt.

"I was just hoping you did," Jennifer explained. "I asked my mother to stay so that she could see how much fun they are and let me have one for my birthday!"

Juanita stood, open-mouthed. "You want a piñata?"

Miguel signaled his mother and pulled her aside. "They can break the piñata I have in my room."

"Miguel, you love that piñata! We brought it all the way from Baja, California. You said you would never break it."

"It's okay, Mom. Truly. Do you have anything to fill it with?"

"I guess I do. I bought my Halloween candy early this year. It should fill the piñata pretty well."

Juanita's mother hung the piñata, which was shaped like a green parrot, in the middle of the patio. Their eyes blindfolded with a scarf, the girls took turns trying to hit the piñata. By pulling on the rope holding it, Juanita's mother moved the piñata up and down, keeping it out of the girls' reach, until Cristina was able to hit it, sending a shower of candy over the girls.

As the girls scrambled to collect the goodies, Samantha announced, "I'm glad I wore a dress, after all," and she held up the edge of her purple skirt, which was filled with candy. She then emptied it on top of the table.

After the girls had shown one another their collection of candies and had finished trading Snickers for Milky Ways, and Life Savers for Chupa-Chups and Gummi Bears, Miguel brought up the cans.

"I have been saving all our empty soft-drink cans for months, just in case someone at this party really wanted to have a good time," he announced.

Sitting in a circle in the floor, the girls played the empty-cans game. With one can in each hand, they first hit them against the floor, then banged the cans against each other, and finally passed the can in their right hand to the person on their right. Faster and faster, around and around they went, all the time singing the traditional song: *Puede usted pasar, pasar sin tropezar* ... You can pass it on, pass it without fumbling ... Soon they decided they could sing other songs, too, and the melodies kept changing as the rhythm went on faster and faster.

Juanita looked around the circle. Jennifer's silky yellow hair bounced, Johnnetta's corn-row braids swung back and forth, Mikaela's sari was mysterious, Victoria's leotards made her look like a dancer, Samantha's party dress looked like fun, and Camille looked so at ease in her jeans.

Maybe what makes a birthday "regular" is to have good fun, she thought, and smiled at Miguel, who winked at her.

Observing the cans she had in her hands, Juanita's thoughts wandered to Bisabuela, her great-grandmother. *Last time we visited her in Florida, Bisabuela said that when she was a little girl in Cuba she used to play this game. Did they have soft-drink cans when Bisabuela was a little girl? What could they have used to play this game?*

Bottles would have been too dangerous.... I guess I'll have to ask her.

Suddenly, Juanita realized that she had lost her concentration and cans were piling up in front of her. All of her friends were giggling and laughing. Then Juanita understood that they had all played a trick on her, so she burst out laughing, too.

"Well, birthday girls, are you all ready for some supper?" Juanita's mother asked.

As she got up from the floor, Juanita wondered if everyone felt as hungry as she did. As she followed her friends to the table, she breathed in deeply the wonderful smells filling the dining room—the spicy curry that Mikaela's mother had cooked, the ginger from the kung pao beef brought by Janice's mom, and the deep and sweet smell of Camille's brownies. Then she recognized, among the others, the familiar aroma of tamales and of her favorite dish, arroz con pollo. Juanita's eyes met her mother's and they both smiled.

The Year We Missed My Birthday

by Amy Goldman Koss

For weeks, my best friend, Nicky, had been nagging me about my birthday. She kept asking me what I wanted to do. I tried to think about it but nothing seemed right.

"You want a regular party?" she asked. "Cake, goodie bags, and all that?"

But I'd been there, done that. Ten times, to be exact.

"Sleepover?" Nicky asked.

I shrugged. A sleepover didn't sound *eleven* to me. And I don't get why Nicky's so hot for sleepovers, anyway. She's scared to death of the dark and hates ghost stories.

"I know!" Nicky called to say. "How 'bout a picnic with a whole bunch of us? Frisbee? Maybe bring our dogs?"

I tried to imagine my fat old Fred jumping into the air for a Frisbee. Picture a leaping sofa.

Bowling was Nicky's next suggestion.

"Ick," I shook my head. "Not bowling."

"Well, how about a movie?" she asked, getting irritated.

We'd gone to the movies for her last birthday, so I just said, "Nah, there's nothing I'm dying to see."

"Fine," Nicky huffed. "If *you* don't care about your stupid birthday, why should *I*?"

And I answered, "You shouldn't."

Period. The end, right? Nope, only the beginning.

Next thing I knew, Nicky blabbed to the entire world that I was refusing to have a birthday this year. In no time the rumor of my canceled birthday clanged down on me like a trap. So, by the time Alison asked me if I was positive I didn't want a party, I couldn't exactly turn around and say, "I never said that! I just didn't want to go bowling!"

And when Danielle said that since I wasn't doing anything on my birthday, she was going to go to her cousin Sarah's for the weekend, what could I say but, "Tell Sarah hi for me"?

The last straw was when Jennifer, the most popular girl in school, spoke to me for the first time in my life to say, "I'm like so totally impressed! I could never in a million years skip my birthday! Aren't you going to miss getting gifts?"

Eew! I hadn't thought about that. But it was too late to do anything but get a grip and pretend I couldn't care less about any of that baby stuff. And, anyway, I really didn't want to go sit in the dark at the movies or make poor old Fred try to chase a Frisbee, not that he would.

Soon, news of my non-birthday spread like the flu, from my school to my house. Here's how: My friends were over when my little sister, Dee, marched into my room, looking fierce. "What's this about you not having a birthday?" she demanded.

"Who told you?" I asked.

And she answered, "EVERYONE, that's who! Is it TRUE?"

But before I had a chance to say anything, Nicky jumped in and said, "It's *totally* true! She won't even let us give her presents!"

And Danielle added, "But if you've already bought her something, Deedles, you can just give it to me."

Ha-ha. Hilarious.

My sister went white and sputtery. I pointed to

my bedroom door and she stumbled out as if she'd been bonged on the head. Birthdays were super-sacred to Dee. In fact, she LIVED for her birthday. She always knew EXACTLY how many months, weeks, and days it was until her next one. And she spent a staggering amount of time planning and replanning each birthday bash. Last year was her Hawaiian luau with green plastic grass skirts, fake coconut bras, and weird pineapple concoctions. The year before we had a house full of giggling girls dressed as mice. Don't ask.

Meanwhile, I wondered how Dee had heard about my non-birthday thing. She didn't even go to my school. Was the entire planet in on this? If you ask me, it was pretty pathetic that nobody had anything better to do than yap about my not wanting to play charades this year.

Then, at dinner, Dee put on her tattle voice to announce to Mom that I wasn't having a birthday party this year.

Mom turned to me and said, "Really?"

Dee answered, "That's what she's telling every-one and everybody thinks she's loony bins! I do! Don't you? It's not right to skip your birthday, is it, Mommy?"

My mom shrugged and said, "I didn't start ig-noring my birthdays till I hit my forties." Then she shook her head and said, "You kids grow up so fast nowadays!"

And that was that.

Later, I overheard her telling my dad that they'd lucked out with my anti-birthday plan because Mom had to be at Dee's soccer playoffs all weekend and Dad had a sales conference that he shouldn't miss.

That night in my room, I tried to discuss the situation with Fred, but he snored through the whole conversation. We didn't know Fred's birthday because he'd been a stray from the pound. But Fred was cool about that kind of thing. He didn't care when he got here; he was just glad to be here now. Especially if there was something in his bowl or if I let him sleep on my bed and hog the pillow.

As the day got closer, I went through all kinds of stuff in my head. Sometimes I was sort of proud and swaggery about being the first kid I knew to outgrow birthday parties, even if I hadn't meant to.

But other times I practically HATED Nicky for stealing my birthday. I wanted to shriek and claw and throw a tantrum-to-end-all-tantrums, insisting that my birthday be returned to me, candles, cake, presents, party, funny hats, dippy song, and all. But I didn't.

And soon, everyone forgot all about it. That is, everyone but my little sister. The *idea* of my skipping a birthday still horrified her beyond words. I suspect Dee was afraid it was contagious and that soon she'd be forced to give up her birthday, too. Maybe it reminded her of when I told her who the tooth fairy was, and took all the fun out of her loose teeth.

The last few days before my birthday, Dee followed me around, saying stuff like, "What are you going to do if Grandma calls to sing you 'Happy Birthday'? Hang up on her?"

And, "What about the blueberry cheesecake?" (My favorite.) "You going to skip that, too? On purpose? Are you NUTS?"

She even tried to make me feel guilty by saying, "Poor Fred loves parties! He'll be so disappointed."

"It's true." My dad laughed, patting Fred's sleepy old head. "He's a real party animal."

"Well, people spill food on the floor at parties," Dee said defensively.

Fred opened one drowsy eye.

The night before my birthday, my sister, not one to give up without a fight, said, "It's not too late! You can still invite Nicky and Danielle and Alison and everyone! Or if you're too embarrassed to admit that you changed your mind, I could call them! I don't mind. I'll say it's gonna be a last-minute surprise party! Hey! That's a GREAT idea, don't you think?"

"No."

"Why not?" Dee asked, stomping her foot.

"Because," I answered.

"Oh, come on!" Dee whined. "Don't be such a poop!"

But I reminded her that she had a soccer tournament all weekend and, anyway, Danielle was out of town.

The truth was that a surprise party didn't sound *so* awful, and I almost hoped that Dee would actually SURPRISE me by pulling one together. But, for one thing, Dee was only eight. For another, I'd told her not to, and, for a third, Danielle really was at her cousin Sarah's.

I wondered if I'd lie awake the night before the actual day, regretting the mess I'd let Nicky trick me into, but I didn't. And that's how I came to wake up alone in the house, with no special treats for breakfast, no one smiling toothy smiles at me, no one handing me gift-wrapped packages with tissue paper and bows, or singing that stupid birthday song to me.

You know how after you're sent sprawling on ice, you sort of think yourself over, checking to see if all your parts work? Arms? Legs? Well, that was what I did in bed that birthdayless morning, asking myself, Am I okay? Sad? Mad?

The answer was hungry. I was definitely hungry.

There was a note on the kitchen table saying that Mom was at my sister's soccer game and that Fred had already been fed. Did I mention that Fred was a little chunky? Okay, not just chunky—he was fat. It turned out that for years, my mom, Dad, Dee, and I had all been feeding him, thinking we were each the only ones. It took the vet telling us that Fred was ready to explode before we figured it out.

I made myself breakfast and read the comics. Not all of them, just *Zits*, *Drabble*, *Fox Trot*, and *For Better or Worse*. Fred laid his big old head in my lap, trying to convince me that Mom's note was a lie. *No one fed me today*, his eyes said, *or yesterday, either!*

I skimmed down to find my astrological forecast at the bottom of the page. There was a special part I'd never noticed before, for people whose birthdays were today. *Hey!* I thought, *that's me!*

My birthday astrology thing didn't make boat-loads of sense, saying I should "stay attuned for a social swell in April" and something about my "busi-ness prospects steering my career in the direction of my dreams through November." But so what if it sounded goony? The point was that people whose birthdays were today had birthdays today, no matter what. And that was a fact printed in the newspaper, right there below the comics. Just like it was a fact that eleven years ago today I went from being unborn to being born, whether I planned to have a party for it or not.

Suddenly, I felt, very, very *eleven*.

To celebrate, I took Fred for a waddle around the block to look at everything with my new, eleven-year-old eyes. It's hard to explain, but it seemed like windshield wipers had swooshed the world clearer and cleaner.

While Fred thoroughly sniffed my neighbor's fence, I realized that THIS would be my birthday for the rest of my life and it didn't matter a twig if other people did or said anything about it.

It was MY birthday, my personal, private birthday, and it would be mine no matter what, forever, even if I lived to be a hundred. In fact, if I chose to celebrate my hundredth birthday, it would be eighty-nine years exactly from TODAY. That thought practically gave me chills, it felt so importantly life and death.

When Fred and I rounded the corner, we saw my mom's car in the driveway. That meant she and Dee were home between soccer matches. Fred picked up his pace in hope of snacks.

We found my mom in the kitchen, unpacking groceries. She lifted a familiar pink bakery box onto the counter and looked apologetically at me. "Blueberry cheesecake," she shrugged. "Sorry, but Dee insisted."

I didn't mind a bit.

Celebration

by Nora Raleigh Baskin

I don't like birthdays. Mine especially. No particular reason. It's just the way I am. I'm not crazy about other people's, either. But I do like a good party. I figured Caroline Prescott was going to have a good birthday party when I opened her invitation and confetti spilled out. Something about all those sparkly, colorful little stars and moons and hearts seemed promising.

I was ever so wrong.

In fact, I've been wrong so many times before, really, I should just expect it.

Like the time I thought (because I had asked him for one) that my father was going to get me a CD player for my birthday, a real CD player with two speakers that I could put on opposite sides of my room. The kind that really belongs in your room, nearly a piece of furniture, something permanent. Something grown-up.

The hardest part was hiding the look on my face when my father gave me my birthday gift. And I opened it.

"Do you like it, sweetie?" my dad asked me.

I choked down my disappointment. It was a CD player but it was small, one square pink box with a plastic handle and vents on each side where the sound came out, almost like a toy. If he had gotten it at a toy store, I wouldn't have been surprised.

"I love it, Dad," I said. I kept my head down like I was reading the box. Really studying it hard. Four D batteries not included. You couldn't even plug it in. Inside the box was a sheet of flower decals you could stick on the sides.

I couldn't hurt my dad. I would never hurt my dad. But it was one of those moments when I thought, *If I had my mother, she'd have gotten me what I wanted*.

She would have known and understood.

Mothers always know.

Fathers don't always get it right.

Very often, they screw it all up. For my eleventh birthday, I had a party of my own. My grandmother, my father's mother, even came up from New York City to help out. I knew I was in trouble when she asked if she could polish my party shoes.

"I don't have party shoes, Nana."

My nana stood about five feet two inches tall, but people said she had great legs and she always looked ready for a night on the town, even at two in the afternoon. She wouldn't leave her house unless she had "put on her face," which meant applying her makeup, which took about an hour and half. Seriously.

"Of course, you do. You must," my grandmother insisted.

I shook my head. I was in sneakers and jeans and planned on staying that way. The ten girls I had invited were due any minute.

"Well, then, what do you wear with your party dress?" she asked me.

Apparently, my dad had left the planning to my grandmother, so we had pin the tail on the donkey, musical chairs (surely the most boring and cruel game ever invented), cake and ice cream. Then, when that was all over, and there was still twenty minutes left, my grandmother made everyone sit in a circle and play telephone. She called it whisper down the lane but it was the same game, where one person says something into the ear of the person next to her, like, "The boy jumped into the pond and started spinning." And so on until the last person says it out loud and it is completely different.

Is this supposed to be fun?

"Toys don't run into a hog unless they're swimming."

Everybody laughed, but I thought surely I was going to die and, if not, I wished I could. I hoped I would not live to see my twelfth birthday.

Except I did. And now Caroline Prescott was having her birthday party.

In a beauty salon.

I could actually feel my body going into shock, which is when your heart starts to beat hard and your ears kind of clog up and you can't think straight. I probably should have given this a little more thought when I RSVP'd Caroline Prescott's birthday party.

"This is it," my dad said when he pulled our car up to the address on the invite. "But it looks like a beauty parlor."

"It is, Dad," I told him, trying to sound casually annoyed instead of terrified.

"Sounds more like an errand, doesn't it? Not a party."

I just got out of the car and ran inside before he could say anything more.

"Libby? Are you listening? You can pick any hairstyle you want," Maggie was saying.

I forced myself to look down at the big book Maggie had on her lap. The truth is, I go into shock fairly easily. But Maggie was my best friend. She wouldn't embarrass me. I took a deep breath.

"I don't know, Mags. What do you think?"

Maggie had a mother named Janie (that's what she liked to be called, even by kids). Maggie had two sisters, three dogs, and a baby brother. So Maggie knew about this kind of stuff. And I had learned it was good to run these things by her before exposing myself to the world. I had once asked Maggie what "training your bangs" meant after I had overheard two girls in middle school discussing this.

I had the funny image of a circus trainer, with whip and chair in hand, beating back someone's unruly hair. And although I knew this probably wasn't what they were talking about, I really had no idea.

Whips and chairs, Maggie explained, was not at all correct. It had to do with getting your hair to fall from one side to another, from a side part or a center part, or none at all, or something like that.

"My hair is too short for any of those hairstyles," I told Maggie. I was trying to concentrate but there was an overwhelming smell in this place. A mixture of shampoo and strong chemicals.

The other girls were dancing all around the room, running from the pyramid stacks of nail polish to rows of hair products. One whole wall was lined with mirrors so they could watch themselves at the same time.

"What about this one?" Maggie pointed to a picture in the book.

"Huh?"

Maggie turned to me. "Libby, what's wrong?"

"I don't know," I said.

I didn't. Not really. I mean, there was the uncomfortable feeling of being in a place I wasn't familiar with. I had never been in a beauty salon. My babysitter had cut my hair in her living room for as long as I could remember. Even after she stopped babysitting, because she got a full-time job as a hairstylist, she still cut both my brother's and my hair in her house for a fraction of what those "rip-off beauty parlors" get. That's how my dad put it, anyway.

I had never gotten a manicure or even used nail polish. I certainly didn't wear makeup, even though most of the "in girls" in my sixth-grade class came to school every day in frosty lip gloss and shimmery eye shadow. Maggie didn't. Her mother wouldn't let her and that was good enough for me.

But it was something else about being here. The smell? The lighting, maybe? It was so bright. There was even music coming from the ceiling. Something else altogether? I couldn't quite figure it out.

"So, girls, which one of you is ready for the hair-stylist?" It was Caroline's mother, Mrs. Prescott.

Always *Mrs.* Prescott. She was standing right in front of Maggie and me, her arms crossed over her chest. I have radar for mothers that aren't going to like me because I am not like their daughters. Right at that moment, the needle on my radar was going crazy.

"Libby can go next," Maggie offered.

I turned and said, "No, you." Too quickly. I think I even pushed Maggie off the couch a little. Mrs. Prescott gave me a look. She definitely didn't like girls who pushed other girls off their seats.

Surely, I didn't belong here.

While some girls were getting their hair done, others were getting manicures and pedicures, and, in the far corner, there was a woman waiting to "put someone's face on."

"Well, then, Libby," Mrs. Prescott said. She pointed. "You can go to the makeup station."

Makeup station?

Maggie looked back at me from the chair where she was now sitting, while a huge black bib was being tied around her neck. She looked like she was getting a massive X-ray at the dentist. There was nothing she could do for me now. She was going to get the "number seven" hairstyle. French braids with ribbon. I bet she was going to look beautiful.

And I was going to the guillotine.

"Come on, now," Mrs. Prescott said. She had her hand on my back that way I really hate, pressing into the center of my spine. "You're way behind."

And you have such a big behind, I thought but didn't say. After Mrs. Prescott had launched me into motion, she wandered off toward the manicure station.

Why don't I like birthdays? I started thinking as I stepped up into the chair. *And why do I always do things I don't want to do?*

Like sitting in this chair. Like being here at this party.

"I'm Melissa," the woman behind me said. She had a nice voice, but she had a big brush in her hand and lots of lipsticks, mascara wands, and long colored pencils on a tray next to her.

I closed my eyes and kept them closed. Okay, I'd let her paint my stupid face with her stupid makeup, but none of it, none of it would help.

"What's your name?" Melissa's voice asked me.

I opened my eyes, but kept them lowered. "Libby," I answered.

"Libby," she said. "That's a wonderful name. Is it short for anything?"

"No, just Libby." Which wasn't exactly true, because I knew I had been named for my mother's mother, Lizbeth, who had died right before I was born. If they had waited a bunch more years, they could have named me after my mother when she died. I could have been Arlene. But, of course, that didn't make any sense.

"What would you like me to do for you, Libby?" she asked me.

Now there's a question.

I let myself glance sideways. Mrs. Prescott was over at the manicure table with Caroline, picking out the perfect color for her daughter—Brazilian Vacation or Sheer Ecstasy?

At that moment, Caroline tossed her head back and laughed that inclusive girly-laugh I never seemed to be included in.

"Nothing," I answered Melissa's question. "I mean, whatever. Whatever you do, I guess."

Melissa smiled. "Well, for the models I work on, I have to cover up all the damage they did the night before. Lack of sleep, too much partying, you know? For some women I try to hide their flaws, a big nose or no cheekbones. For some girls, I try to accentuate their good points."

She put her hands on my head and pulled my hair off my forehead. Her hands felt soft and smelled like flowers in a garden, and oranges.

"Maybe a little eyeliner and some lip gloss," Melissa said. "Would you like that?"

I shrugged and looked away. I didn't want to see myself in the mirror. I couldn't understand why I was feeling the way I was. It surrounded me and separated me from everyone else in the room, like music that only I was hearing.

"You're very pretty, you know," Melissa was saying. "A natural beauty. You have great skin. You're so lucky . . ." She was going on while she dabbed at my eyelids. At the same time, she was touching my face, holding my chin in her hands, gently.

In the mirror I could see my own face, plain and kind of sad. I could see Melissa standing behind me, her hand still stroking my hair back. It felt good, but a deep well of loneliness was creeping up and all around me.

No, I don't know that, I wanted to tell her. I don't know that I'm pretty.

Am I?

I mean, my dad told me I was pretty all the time, but he was my dad and so he had to say that. My grandmother said the same thing, but she thought those fake-looking salesladies on the shopping channel were the most beautiful women in the world.

If my mother were alive, she'd tell me I was beautiful. Wouldn't she?

Would I believe her?

"Now, go like this," Melissa said. She made a popping noise with her lips so I did the same. I could feel the sticky lip gloss. I wondered how I was going to be able to eat birthday cake.

"Look up, silly." Melissa walked over and straightened the mirror so it was directly in front of me. "Look at yourself," Melissa said.

I didn't want to, and that's when I knew why I didn't like birthdays, not mine and not anyone else's. Because I was always disappointed. I would never have a birthday like other girls had birthdays. I would never have someone like Mrs. Prescott flying around, making sure everything went just right for her daughter, making sure the whole world stopped just because it was Caroline's birthday. I didn't like birthdays because—

Because I was jealous.

I looked up into the mirror before me.

"Look how beautiful you are," Melissa said.

I wasn't beautiful. I was jealous and jealousy was ugly. Whatever Melissa was talking about I wasn't seeing it. I felt like I was going to cry.

"Girls, girls, girls." It was Mrs. Prescott's loud voice. "Now, make sure your nails are dry. Don't muss up your marvelous hairdos, don't smudge your makeup."

What kind of words are smudge and muss, I thought.

"It's almost time to open the presents," Mrs. Prescott finished her announcement.

I squeezed my eyes shut again. I didn't want the tears to come. *Not now. Please, not now.*

"You look great, Libby." Maggie came up behind me. I turned around. Her hair was all braided and interlaced with white ribbon. She did look beautiful.

I should have told her that, but I didn't. For some reason, I couldn't. Melissa patted me on the shoulders and I slid off the stool.

"Thank you," I whispered to her.

"Anytime," Melissa said.

Some of the girls were starting to get a little wild, especially Madison Gladstone, who was getting a running start and then sliding across the smooth slippery floor. I guess her nails were dry enough and she wasn't particularly worried about smudging her makeup.

"I really don't think that is a very good idea," the manicure lady was saying. She was probably much madder than that, but I suppose she didn't know whether Madison was the birthday girl or not. Only nothing was stopping Madison.

Instead she was joined by Jordan Makish, and now they were both gliding dangerously close to the table with the pot of paraffin wax. The manicure lady was looking back and forth, desperately looking for Mrs. Prescott, I figured.

"Wheeew . . . ," Madison shouted.

"Whoopee." Jordan slid right by me. Her pile of hair extensions and silver beads was definitely getting mussed.

By the time Mrs. Prescott noticed all this extremely unsalonlike behavior, it was too late, but it really wasn't Jordan's or Madison's fault. It was Caroline's.

"Stop, you guys." Caroline took two steps and stood directly in the line of Jordan's projected path. She held up her hand like a traffic cop. "You're ruining my whole party."

To her credit, Jordan tried to slow down, but Madison was right behind her. Jordan slid slowly to a stop, but when she was banged directly in the back by Madison, she careened into the three-legged table of paraffin wax. The legs of the table gave way, and the pot of wax teetered to the edge, where it balanced for a fraction of a second and then dropped onto the floor.

"This is the worst birthday ever," Caroline's voice sounded above everything and had the effect of quieting the whole room. She even stamped her foot. "It's totally ruined."

"No, no, Caroline. It's fine," her mother said. She wrapped her arm around her daughter and then looked over to the upturned table and now rolling pot of wax. "I'll take care of that. I'll take care of everything."

I was amazed at how fast a pot of wax can actually roll and how fast Mrs. Prescott could move.

"It's fine. See, it's all fine," she announced. She picked up the pot. "It wasn't turned on. It didn't even spill."

Caroline did not seem the least bit relieved. She stamped her foot again. "Everyone hates my party," she whined.

"No, no. They're just full of energy," Mrs. Prescott was saying. "They're all just hungry. I'll get the veggies and dip."

Jordan and Madison were still kneeling on the floor, seeming not sure of what to do now. Then, suddenly, they stood up, and all at once, like a flock of birds in motion, all the girls ran over to tell Caroline what a wonderful party it was. The greatest idea. The most fun. The best birthday party ever.

The best.

"Wanna get out of here for a minute?" Maggie asked me. She didn't wait for an answer. She took my hand and we stepped outside the glass front door. Together and without a word, we both sat down on the steps. It was autumn chilly, but the air felt freeing and I could finally breathe.

"Some party, huh?" Maggie said.

"I shouldn't have come," I said.

"You say that at every birthday party." Maggie looked right at me. "Even mine."

"I did not," I said. "Never."

Maggie had her knees up to her chin. "You didn't have to. I knew."

I tried to remember Maggie's last birthday party. It would have been at her house, like all her parties, but there wouldn't have been musical chairs or whistle down the lane. Maggie's birthday is in the summer. Now I remembered. We played water-balloon toss and ran under the sprinkler. There was a table set up outside with bowls of nuts, and crushed Oreos, and marshmallow, and caramel for make-your-own-sundaes. Her mother didn't care when we tracked dirt and grass into the house.

"Don't worry. That's why the mop was invented," her mother had said, laughing.

"I liked your party," I said.

"Maybe, but you didn't have a good time."

"I didn't?"

Maggie shook her head.

"I wanted to."

"I know," Maggie said. We could hear Mrs. Prescott

inside. It sounded as if she had regained some kind of order. It must be gift-opening or vegetable-dipping time.

"We better go in," I said.

"We don't have to," Maggie said. "If you don't want to."

"No, it's okay now. But you know what I was thinking?"

"No. What?"

We both stood up at the exact same time. Maggie and I did everything the same. We had been best friends since second grade, the year before my mother died. She was the only one of my friends who had known my mother. She was the only one who could remember her and we were both beginning to forget. I had to look at pictures now, just to remember what my mother looked like.

"Well, anyone can be born, right?" I started. I didn't know where I was going with this. It was just the beginning of a thought, a feeling.

"Yeah?"

"I mean, it doesn't take anything to be born. You don't even know you're doing it. You don't even have much to do with it, I don't think. Right?"

"That's true," Maggie answered. "My mother says it took seventeen hours for her to have me. I don't think I had anything to do with it."

I liked that Maggie was never afraid to mention her own mother in front of me.

"Well, so, maybe birthdays aren't such a big deal," I said. "It's not being born that's such a big deal. It's all the living you have to do afterwards."

Maggie looked like she was really listening. Then, slowly, she nodded and somehow I knew that what I was saying was very, very true.

"That's the hard part," I went on. "I mean, they should have a party for that. For just living. Every day."

"We should," Maggie agreed. She smiled at me.

Yes, I thought. Someday we would celebrate.

Someday.

Very soon.

Happy Birthday to Hugh

by Lois Metzger

Nola was the new kid. Everybody else had been at school half a year already. She was the only sixth grader who didn't know where the art studio was, and who always got lost on the third floor, looking for the bathroom.

"It's your birthday soon!" her mother had said. "Why not have a big party this year, invite a whole bunch of new friends?"

Back in her old school, in her old neighborhood, Nola had had a best friend, Sandy, who, like Nola, was happy to have one friend and not one hundred, happy to have a tiny birthday party, just the two of them, a trip to the zoo and ice cream after. Nola didn't always listen to her mother's advice. But now, in the middle of the school year, such an awkward time for her father to switch jobs and move the family, she felt kind of raw, and her mother's words echoed in her head.

"Keep your eyes open," her mother had told her. "See who all the girls flock to. Try to become her friend, and the rest will follow."

Finding that girl was easy. Getting close to her was not. Courtney was always surrounded by a dozen girls, like she was on a trampoline and they were spotting her. In the school play, *Romeo and Juliet*, she was Juliet. On the basketball team she scored more points than girls in the eighth grade. And she was in the after-school science club, headed by Mr. Frank, the most popular teacher, who had a gray ponytail and told stories that everyone laughed at.

Nola had come to school too late to try out for the play or the basketball team. But science had always been her best subject, so she joined the science club. Still, Courtney didn't pay much attention to her, even when Nola thought of putting a battery-operated hair dryer in the ash volcano. It spectacularly blew out thick clouds of gray ash. Mr. Frank was impressed.

"I got the ash from my fireplace," Courtney told him.

"The hair dryer was brilliant," he said.

"It was a group project," Courtney explained.

But now, on this fiercely cold January afternoon, just before school ended, Courtney pulled Nola aside. "I've got a fantastic idea!" she said. "Tomorrow is Mr. Frank's birthday! Let's get him a card. At science club, we can pass it around secretly, sign it, and give it to him right before club starts. He doesn't know that I know. I heard him telling the art teacher. He'll be so shocked! I can't wait to see his face!"

"That's a fantastic idea," Nola agreed. *It's my birthday in three weeks*, she thought but didn't say. *I don't know what to do for it. Should I have a big party? Do you have any fantastic ideas for me about that?*

"Problem is," Courtney said, "I don't have time to go to the store. Do you mind, Nola? Michael can't go—he's got basketball. As for Judd—he's out sick or something. Not that I'd want to get close enough to even *ask* him. He's gross."

Judd was tall and lanky and had stringy hair and a unibrow. Nola had already noticed that no one wanted to get close to him.

"Now pick out a cute one, nothing gross."

"Oh, I wouldn't—"

"I know! I'm kidding!"

But Nola could tell that Courtney was deadly serious. Nola saw how Courtney soaked up the details of Mr. Frank's life, which he tossed out during science club. He liked backpacking, and Mexican food, and vintage cars he could buy cheap and fix up. He called Courtney "Juliet," because of the play and, when he did, she smiled as if, like Juliet, she really was the sun.

"This is so nice of you, Nola. Thank you so much!" Courtney dashed off, and a bunch of girls rushed up as she was dashing. The girls who Nola's mother wanted to invite to a big birthday party. Some of them were so volcanic—they loved one another and just as suddenly hated one another. Calm and easy one moment, and spewing out thick gray ash the next.

"Now, don't forget!" Courtney called over her shoulder.

"I won't," Nola said. "I don't forget things so easily." As Nola watched Courtney walk down the hall, the other girls told her, "Call me later!"

"I will!" Courtney promised.

Wait a minute. If Courtney had time to call them, didn't she have time to pick up a card?

Just after winter vacation, Courtney had celebrated her own twelfth birthday by inviting all the sixth-grade girls, even Nola, who had only just arrived at school, over for dinner and a sleepover. They went to a restaurant with a karaoke machine. Nola joined in the backup on a couple of songs—it was fun, she had a good time. *Should I have a party like this?* she wondered. She and Sandy loved the zoo, especially in sub-zero February, when nobody else was around and they didn't have to wait in long lines to see the baby gorillas. At Courtney's party, all the girls spread out sleeping bags in a shaggy carpet, and talked about their goals in life. Courtney wanted to be an actress—"if only I wasn't so gross," she said.

"You're gorgeous!" the other girls assured her.

"I'm gross," Courtney insisted, while the girls pointed out her beautiful green eyes, her wavy, waist-length, reddish brown hair, her perfect skin that never saw a pimple.

"I want to be a spokesperson," another girl, Kimberly, said.

"A spokesperson for what?" Nola asked.

"It doesn't matter. But if somebody has something to say, I can be the one to say it."

Another girl wanted to be a United Nations ambassador for peace; still another saw herself running a company. Nola had been self-conscious even before it was her turn, wearing a long nightgown with horses on it—last year's birthday gift from Sandy, who had one just like it. All the other girls wore tank tops with matching silky pants, or little slips with lacy collars. Nola had long braids. The other girls had loose, fluffy hair. It was at that moment Nola decided she would go to Sassy Cuts and cut off her braids. And in the next moment she turned back to the conversation. "A veterinarian," she said. "I really like animals." The other girls exchanged looks, so she blurted out, "Or maybe an astronomer."

"How about a veterinarian in outer space?" Kimberly said, laughing at her own joke.

"Oh, Kimmy, that joke—it's so not working for you," Courtney said, and everyone else laughed—including Nola, who didn't really feel like laughing. Kimberly got mad and wouldn't watch the movie they'd rented, but later she and Courtney highlighted each other's hair. One of the girls, Alex, made a point of telling Nola during the movie that she liked animals, too.

Nola stood in the card store for a half hour, trying to find something "cute, not gross."

Sleep When You're Dead! one of them said, with a picture of a cemetery. *Live it Up!*

That was dumb. So many of them were so dumb.

Only 365 Days Until Your Next Birthday! Make it a Good One! and *It's Your Birthday—Have a Blast!* That one had a beautiful photograph of a star going super-nova. Actually, she liked this card, but not for Mr. Frank. She kept looking.

How Are Birthdays Like Garden Weeds? They Keep Creeping Up on You!

That sounded more like Mr. Frank.

At dinner that night, Nola's mother said, "How's it going at school?"

"Mm," Nola replied.

"Have you gotten friendly with any of the girls yet?"

All Nola could do was shrug her shoulders.

"Well, I was talking to Cindy Green today," her mother continued. "She has a daughter in your grade. I think her name is Kimberly. She said Kimberly's always so busy, either on the phone, or out at some 'group thing'—"

"Courtney asked me to get a birthday card for a teacher," Nola broke in. "She was really nice, when she was asking me."

"Speaking of birthdays—"

"Leave her alone," her father cut in.

"You don't understand," her mother said. "You were a *boy*. It can be very lonely for a girl."

Nola thought of Judd. He seemed pretty lonely, for someone who wasn't a girl.

"It's just something I've come to learn, Nola. It's better to have lots of friends. I had one friend, just like you and Sandra. We had a huge fight and never spoke again."

"Mom, Sandy and I don't have fights. We still IM each other every night—"

"I think you're missing my point. There's safety in numbers, that's my point."

"Mom, 'safety in numbers' refers to the fact that herbivores live in large groups so any one of them is less likely to get picked off by a predator."

"I don't see how herbs have anything to do with anything—"

"Leave her alone," her father repeated. "It's a new school. Let her figure out how she fits in. Let her figure out what kind of birthday she wants."

Nola liked the sound of that.

"Of course," her mother said. "I'm only suggesting—wait, don't eat the peas yet!"

Her father held a forkful of peas halfway to his lips.

"I microwaved them. It hasn't been five minutes."

Nola's mother had this thing about food that had been microwaved. She'd read somewhere that when it comes out of the microwave, it's still cooking for five minutes. If you eat it too soon, it sits in your stomach, cooking. Nola wasn't sure this was true, but she stared at her peas and waited for them to stop. Who wanted something still cooking inside you?

Courtney frowned at the card.

"Is it okay?" Nola said.

Courtney smiled and flipped back her hair. "It's fine." She reached into her locker, took out a pen, and wrote, "Happy Birthday to a super guy! From Juliet."

Michael came up to them. He was long and lean, and, even when he wasn't shooting a basket, always seemed to be in motion. He'd joined the science club because he needed some extra credit. "What's that? Oh, yeah, the card for Mr. Frank. Courtney told me." He wrote, "Happy Birthday from Michael." And he frowned, too. "Garden weeds? I don't get it."

"They creep up on you. Like birthdays."

"I turned twelve in December. Nothing creepy about that."

"Not *creepy*. A birthday might *creep up*. When you're older, you get so caught up in things, you might even forget your birthday. Not like when you're a kid and it's all you think about."

Michael nodded in rhythm, maybe to a song in his head. "If you say so," he said, not looking too convinced.

"See, that's my issue with the card," Courtney said. "Mr. Frank is a very youthful person."

"You said it was fine," Nola said.

"Well, too late to change it now!"

It was Nola's turn. She scribbled out, "Sleep when you're dead! Live it up! From Nola." Right away she wished she could take it back, write something else, but, as Courtney said, too late to change it now. She stuck it inside the envelope.

"Nola, you need to get Judd to sign it," Courtney said.

There was Judd down the hall, by the water fountain. A calculator in his back pocket stuck out, about to fall.

"Here's the birthday card." Nola handed it to him.

As he straightened up to take it, his calculator fell out with a clack. He looked down at it, then back at Nola. "It's okay—it's unbreakable. Very hard plastic," he said.

"Oh—that's good."

"It's nicer," he said.

"What—the calculator?"

"Your hair."

"Oh, thanks." He was the only one who'd noticed she'd cut off her long braids and now had short curls.

"You look like that girl on *Deep Space Nine*. I've got the whole series on DVD."

"I—what?"

"She was a trill. She hosted people inside her body. It's a little hard to explain."

What was he talking about?

"It's hard, isn't it?"

"What's hard?" Was he still talking about that girl with people in her body?

"Being the new kid."

"Oh." He was the only one who'd noticed this, too. "It's okay." She added, "And sometimes not okay."

"I know. Teachers stand you up in front of the classroom and introduce you. And they think, that's that. But sometimes that isn't that."

Well. Now she knew exactly what he was talking about.

In the classroom, Courtney and Michael were joking about whether to sing, "Happy Birthday to You" or "Happy Birthday to Hugh." Hugh was Mr. Frank's first name. "So, where's the card?" Courtney asked.

"Judd has it."

"What, is he searching his nerd brain for something clever to say?" She laughed.

"I didn't want to stand there, watching him. Let him have some privacy."

"Oh, please. Nola, you need to get it. Mr. Frank will be here any minute."

Nola went out to the hall. "Judd?"

"Yeah?"

"You have the card, right?"

"Yeah, you gave it to me!" He took a step closer. He smelled like a wet sweater, though he had on only a T-shirt. "Thanks so much, you guys. That was so cool. I appreciate it so much."

"What?" Nola said.

"How'd you know it was my birthday? It's not until next week, but better early than never, right? Or, is it, better late than never?"

"Better late," Nola said. What was going on here?

"It was so cool. 'Sleep when you're dead! Live it up!'" He laughed. There was a kind of light in his eyes, under that unibrow.

Because he thought the card was for him.

Nola remembered what everyone had written. Nowhere was Mr. Frank's name. Not even on the envelope. Judd thought the card was for him and there was no evidence to prove him wrong.

"So, when's your actual birthday?" she asked.

"January nineteenth."

"You're . . . three weeks older than me."

"Those three weeks have taught me a lot! Respect your elders!" He thought this was hilarious.

Nola rushed back into the classroom.

"Well?" Courtney said.

"Judd thinks the card is for him."

"No way." Courtney dismissed this with a wave of her hand. "It's for Mr. Frank."

"Judd doesn't know that! He kept thanking me." *There was a light in his eyes,* Nola wanted to say.

"Look," Courtney said, "I would never tell Judd what a super guy he is and sign it 'Juliet.' What if he starts showing it around? I'll die!" She didn't look like she was going to die. She just looked mad. "You should have told Judd, 'This is Mr. Frank's card. Sign it.' Why didn't you?"

"I don't know. I guess I forgot he was out yesterday." But Nola didn't forget things so easily. At least, not until now.

"Well, somebody's got to straighten this out. Nola?"

Nola just stood there.

Courtney smiled warmly. "It's actually pretty funny, don't you think? Judd's so gross, Mr. Frank's so awesome ... you know, I'm having some kids come for a sleepover this weekend. You could come, too, and tell everybody all about it!"

So, this was her ticket *in.* Nola pictured herself at Courtney's—wearing new pajamas this time, really cute ones, like something one of the other girls had worn at the party, a flowery camisole top, wide-leg pants, and a matching bandanna. She could hear them laughing. *Did Judd really think that? What did he say? Nola, that's hysterical!* Friends, lots of them, friends she could invite to her own big birthday party....

So why did Nola feel all eaten up inside, like she'd eaten microwaved peas too soon?

"Let it go," she heard herself say.

"What?" said Courtney, sharp as an icy wind.

"Let Judd keep it. He doesn't get too many birthday cards, clearly."

"It's not Judd's card." Courtney sounded as if she was explaining something very simple to a very young child. "It belongs to Mr. Frank."

"Let it go," Nola said, even louder this time—and with that, she knew, she was letting it all go, the sleepovers at Courtney's, the safety in numbers, the matching bandanna.

Judd came into the room. He smiled. These were his friends. They'd gotten him a birthday card. A little early, but that was okay—

"There you are!" Courtney smiled, too. "Nola gave you a card. Maybe there was a misunderstanding somewhere? It's for Mr. Frank. Nola wanted you to sign it. Have you signed it?"

Nola watched Judd's eyes, under that unibrow. He looked confused. But only for a moment. The card wasn't for him. It had never been for him. The light vanished. Now there was a hurt in his eyes. Nola never saw anything like it. Like his heart was one big calculator, adding up all the hurts in his life.

"Oh, the card," Judd said lightly. "I stuck it in my locker. By mistake. Be right back." And he left.

"Good." Courtney flipped back her hair. "That's done."

Mr. Frank got his card. He smiled at it. "You kids are *da bomb*!" he said. He put it facedown on his desk, so carelessly it almost fell off. He told a story about how he couldn't start his 1955 Chevrolet that morning. Courtney laughed and laughed.

Nola decided to get Judd a birthday card—the super-nova one. And she'd write a nice message. Something real. She still wasn't sure what to do about her own birthday. Not a big party. But a party sounded good. With Sandy, of course, and maybe Alex, too, that girl from Courtney's party, the one who liked animals. A party for three—why not?

They all gathered around Mr. Frank and sang "Happy Birthday"—Judd loudest of all, off-key.

With Love, From Mom and Dad

by Rita Williams-Garcia

"If I don't like him," I boasted, "I can call off the engagement."

"Medha, your father would freak," Geeta said.

"And your mother would cry," Ratna chimed in.

"My mother would do more than cry," I agreed. "But I have the last word. If I don't like him, that's it. No deal. No engagement."

We were supposed to prepare for our Spanish quiz at Geeta's. All we could do was talk about my birthday-slash-engagement party. I only had Geeta and Ratna to talk about it with. Although their families weren't very traditional, they were from India, like my family. An arranged engagement was nothing unusual.

"I wonder what his family will bring you," Ratna said. She was so bad. We'd never be ready for the quiz at this rate.

Geeta was no better. "I wonder what they'll bring— besides Amit!"

I tried to seem annoyed with them and serious about the Spanish quiz, but that was a good question. I wondered what Amit's family thought I was worth. Instead, I said, "It could be a brand-new car that sits in the garage until I'm sixteen, for all I care. If I don't like Amit, I can say 'No deal. No engagement.'"

They laughed at me because they knew I cared. Amit's family better bring something great. Something outrageous. Or else.

"Your dad isn't like mine," Geeta said.

"Nor like mine," Ratna said.

Both Geeta and Ratna turned thirteen this year, but neither were engaged. Their parents didn't believe in arranged engagements. They felt their daughters were too young to even think of becoming engaged.

My father felt Geetna and Ratna's parents had lived here in this country too long. My mother said it was their way of saving face. Neither Geeta nor Ratna's parents knew good families to make the proper match, and neither could afford to host an engagement party.

I didn't want my friends to think my parents were too pleased to get rid of me. I insisted, "My parents say it's up to me. I don't have to accept Amit or his family."

"Medha, you're dreaming," Geeta said.

"Dream on," Ratna added.

"You'll see," I told them. "I'm my father's little lichee fruit. I can do what I want."

"Wake up, Medha," Geeta said. "Your mother ordered a lot of food for your party. All my mom talks about are the cakes. How elaborate. How many. Do you think they're having this party so you can say 'no' to Amit's family?"

"Wake up, Medha."

I forgot about Geeta and Ratna. My mother said they'd stick me with little pins of jealousy every chance they got. After all, what did they have for their thirteenth birthdays? A bowling party and a pizza party. It didn't matter. I knew deep down what was what. Geeta and Ratna were still my friends. They wouldn't dream of missing my party.

My mother and I picked up my outfit from the dressmaker. A turquoise salwar set. The neckline, sleeves, and bottom of the tunic were trimmed in silver. The pants, also trimmed in silver. I chose a delicate stole made of a crushed silver tissue with knotted turquoise tassels on the ends. To make my outfit complete, I found the ideal mojaris that fit my feet perfectly. They were silver, to match my outfit, covered in blue glass beads, with a heart-shaped pattern at the big toe.

I never thought I'd hear myself say it, but I was beat from shopping. Just my luck, my mother always got a second wind if something pretty in a store window caught her eye. We couldn't pass a dress shop or shoe shop without Mom saying, "Oh, look! Let's try that on."

My mother loved to give big parties for no reason. Just imagine my birthday party! People would be talking about it for days afterwards. Weeks, even. My mother and my aunts spent months planning it. The food. The clothes. The music. She especially enjoyed dictating designs to the dressmaker and picking out fabric. I'm surprised my mother didn't own dress shops. She thought up dress designs every day. She'd have them made, wear them once, then give them to her sisters. I usually took the accessories she no longer wanted. The mojaris, silk stoles, and jewelry. After all, my mother dresses like a married woman, and I dress like a girl. I might be practically engaged, but I don't see myself having coffee with my mother and the other married women, talking about husbands and households.

Besides, I have years before I marry. If I marry. There's no rush. Most of my cousins were engaged at thirteen or fourteen, but married after college. I could marry after I finish high school or college. Whichever I choose. I guess.

I let out a big sigh when we came inside the house.

My mother laughed at me. "That was fun!" she said.

"My feet are killing me," I complained. I pulled off my sneakers and tossed the shopping bag from the dressmaker on the floor.

My mother picked up the bag and shook her finger at me. "What will you do when you have to clean up after everyone?"

"I'll train everyone to clean up after themselves," I answered.

"Start with yourself. Brat."

My mother and I are so much alike, or so my aunts say. We are both our father's favorite. She got away with doing nothing while her sisters helped their mother around the house. I barely make my bed.

My mother smiled and sat on the sofa with me. Gazing at her, I said to myself, "I have nothing to worry about. My mother is an older married woman, and she is still beautiful." I'm convinced I'll never be old or ugly.

"I want to give this to you before your party. With everyone showering you with presents, I don't want our gift to be lost in the excitement."

Suddenly, I came back to life. "What? What?"

She placed a small box in my hands. I opened it and found two gold bangles, dotted with red gem-stones. Rubies!

"With love, from Mom and Dad," she said.

They were rubies, I thought. I took off my sterling silver bangles and slid my gold bangles on my wrist. The gold band and deep red stones were perfect against my skin.

I hugged my mother. The bangles were stunning. No one at school had anything as spectacular as these.

"Wait until Geeta and Ratna see them."

My mother made a sound. "Be careful with your friends. It will be hard enough for them to come to your party and see how your parents love and spoil you."

Saturday night came quickly enough. I was thirteen, dressed, and made up with blue eyeliner to match my clothes. My family and friends were calling for me but I couldn't bring myself to leave my room. I didn't know why I couldn't enjoy my party. It was lively on the other side of the door. The music was going. The guests were all laughing. I could smell the food, but I wasn't hungry.

Finally, Geeta and Ratna arrived, and I let them in my room. They screamed as soon as they saw my bangles.

"This is twenty-four carat!" Geeta cried. "I know twenty-four carat."

"And rubies," Ratna said. "Awesome."

"They're only bangles," I said. "No big deal."

I thought I would enjoy Geeta and Ratna fussing over my things, but I couldn't get into the spirit. "Is anyone missing me?" I asked sheepishly.

"They're too busy enjoying the food. There's enough to feed a country," Geeta said. "Your mother's crazy. You should see all the food."

"Please," I said. "Don't say food. I'll be sick. Really sick."

"What's wrong, Medha? Go out and enjoy your party."

I kept twisting the silver stole. The fabric was so delicate. Why did I choose such a silly thing? "Is Amit's family here?" I asked.

"We don't know what he looks like," Ratna said.

"Go and find out for me. Then come back. Use the

special knock." I should have felt badly about ordering my friends around, but I didn't. "Go! Go!"

I sat curled in a ball on my bed and waited for my friends to return. Finally, there was the special knock. Two fast, pause, followed by two more knocks. I opened the door slightly so no one else could see me. Geeta and Ratna hurried inside, and we shut the door. Their eyes were wide, maybe with terror.

"What? What? You better tell me!"

"Medha, Medha," Geeta began.

"He's ugly!" Ratna blurted.

"No!" I stamped my feet. "No!"

"He is shorter than Geeta."

"And his nose," Geeta said. "There's something odd about it. Don't you think, Ratna?"

"Totally."

I sank down on my bed. "No, no!" I said, over and over. "My parents wouldn't do that to me. They know how I am. They know I won't want an ugly boy to one day be my husband."

"At least the zits will go away," Ratna said.

"Zits?"

"Maybe it's good he has a big nose. You almost forget about the zits."

Zits. Strange nose. Troll. I was almost in tears, but I didn't want to cry and mess up my blue eyeliner.

I tore off a turquoise tassel from the stole. "I can't believe my parents would do this to me. I can't believe it!"

"You know what you have to do," Geeta said. "Tell your father 'no engagement.'"

"That's right, Daddy's Little Lichee Fruit. Say 'Daddy, no deal.'"

"You jealous pig. You think I won't do it, but I will."

"In front of everyone?"

"In front of your parent's friends?"

"Don't dare me. I will."

Geeta opened the door. Ratna said, "Go. Do it."

I went through the door, pushing through the crowds to find my parents. The house was filled with people. They all wanted to greet and shower me with attention, but I was too angry to truly hear or see them. I spotted my father talking to a group of men. I didn't know them, and guessed they were men from Amit's family. How could these tall men produce a troll?

My mother was making her way to me, but she was blocked by groups of people. The largest group, a swarm of girls, gathered around a guy. The guy in the center of the girls turned his head to me. I felt compelled to get a better look, but Geeta and Ratna kept urging me toward my father. Then I became angry again, and remembered how my father betrayed me. It was his idea to pick out the pimply troll, who was probably one of his customer's sons.

My mother waved her hand, trying to get my attention, but Geeta and Ratna kept chanting, "Daddy, no deal. Daddy, no deal," and "Zit Face, Zit Face."

There were too many people standing around me, talking at me, pushing me. My face was feeling hot.

Somehow, my mother maneuvered her way through the guests and was right there. Her hands felt cool on my arm.

"Geeta, Ratna. I hope you brought your parents," Mom greeted them. "I'm sure they would like to enjoy a special occasion for a change."

They giggled. "Great party."

"Medha. Good! It's time to meet Amit's family," she said, turning in the direction of the guy. The one with girls surrounding him.

"Which one is Amit?" I asked her.

By this time, Geeta and Ratna had run off to look for their parents.

"Do not look interested. He's an even bigger brat than you," Mom said.

I tried not to look in his direction, but from a glimpse I could see he was as tall as my father, and his nose looked normal. I didn't want to be caught staring but I was sure that his skin was smooth. Maybe even perfect.

I collected myself and took a deep breath. Our home was filled with people and they had all come to celebrate with me. I smiled and let my guests greet me properly and make as big a fuss as they pleased. After all, Amit had to know that I was the prize. Not he.

Sez You

by Norma Fox Mazer

I ran away on my birthday. And some people said mean things to me after, like Autumn my sister, but not Beauty my sister or Mim my sister, but Faithful my sister she yelled and Mama cried again and and and—

Whoa, girl!

I said that to myself.

I got mixed up and when I get mixed up, I have to go back to Go, like in Monopoly which is my favorite game in the world because I can be a rich person in Monopoly and have houses, red houses and green houses and the red houses are my favorite houses, and I can also count to five hundred and five hundred is a lot of money, and if you don't believe me, you can ask Mim my sister, who teaches me a lot of stuff, which I can remember mostly—

Whoa, girl!

I got mixed up again in what I'm saying.

Go back to Go, Fancy. One thing at a time, Fancy. That is the way I talk to myself, and that is one of the things people say to me when I get mixed up. Take it slow, Fancy. Stick to the point, Fancy.

The point I will stick to is I ran away on my birthday, which is a poem, get it? Poems make me laugh. But it wasn't a joke. And some people, like Autumn my sister who can be MEAN, said I did that run away because I am slow.

But that is a big fat Autumn LIE, which is not a nice word.

But slow is wrong, because I am not slow.

I am the most best excellent fastest running runner in my class. Ha ha! That's a half way joke because who would be a walking runner? I am not like Randy in my class who can never see a joke. See, a joke is also funny and I like funny things.

Funny things are my favorite things in the whole world, which is big, and Mallory where I live is small says Mim my sister, but I don't think so. I think Mallory is big with a lot of streets and stores and houses and cars and big buildings like the opera house which is where people used to get up on the stage and sing, and I think I would like to do that, because I like singing, but Mama makes me stay home and on our street all the time, except when I go to school. Because she says she worries about me and I give her gray hair. But she puts stuff on her hair from the drugstore and it isn't gray, it's black and sometimes it's red, and I laugh when she says gray hair.

I have a big sense of fun. I even have a funny bone in my elbow, which everybody has, but my dad, Mr. Huddle Herbert, says I have a very big funny bone. He's a funny guy. I always laugh when I see my dad, and especially if he says things like Come on, girls, punch me in the belly, it's all muscle, and we all run and punch him and he pretends he's all groany and sorry he asked us, so he's just funny, but not my mama. She's not a funny guy, which is a halfway funny thing, too, because she's a lady, not a guy.

But why I ran away on my birthday is not because she's a lady and it is not because I am slow. I will tell you why.

I ran away because my mama is always sad on my birthday. She cries and cries and cries. Mim my sister told me Mama is remembering the tiny twin babies, Clarity my sister and Charity my sister, who are dead. They got dead on my seven year old birthday and they were four months old and got dead from something bad like Ace flu I think it's called.

There are things I don't understand, like why they got dead. Which makes people sad and cry. But I know how to think about some things like running away. I got prepared. I put a banana in my knapsack and my flashlight and my clock and a book because I know how to read and I love a book called *Why Do Kittens Purr*, but it was too big for my knapsack so I put in another book, which is called *Kiss the Cow*. And I love this book too because it is so funny but I would never kiss a cow. And that is not a lie.

Lying is not a good thing. Mrs. Sokolow my teacher I love says some things are good and some things are bad, and she says, Fancy, good for you, you are a pretty good thinker. Which rhymes with stinker. A stinker thinker!

I don't remember my baby twin sisters but my mama does and my birthday makes her cry because it is their death day, and I ran away so she wouldn't cry. Now I am thirteen and that is a big girl, big enough to run away because I don't want my mama to be sad.

And that is not a lie. I do not tell lies. I tell the truth.

I ran away to the South Street Market, which is

on Market Street—isn't that funny? A market on Market Street?—and I sat down and first I ate my banana, because I was hungry, because it's a pretty long walk to the South Street Market, which is a big long building with a lot of stores inside and Mama drove to it with me three times, and I remembered the streets to go on. One thing I am so good at is remembering streets. Anyone can ask me where is a street and what is the next street and I will tell them. And I like to tell people things and answer questions.

So I was happy when a lady stopped right by me and she was wearing a floppy red hat, and she said Honey, is there a place called Barry's here? And then she spelled it. B.A.R.R.Y. And I said Thank you, but I know how to spell that word. And I spelled it for her. B.A.R.R.Y. And she said Oh never mind. And I didn't. I didn't mind.

And that is one of the words that make me laugh. Because there is your mind which is in your brain which is under your hair which is under your hat if you are wearing one like that lady. And Mim my sister has a very good mind but it's never under a hat because she doesn't like to wear hats, she says her head gets too hot, and maybe that's because she has so many brains. And Beauty my sister has a pretty good mind and she makes funny faces. And Autumn my sister is sometimes mean and sometimes nice and Faithful my sister, she screams and has a bad temper. And I usually don't run away. I usually mind my mother, see that's another mind. But I think oh never mind is the funniest because how can you never mind if you have a mind?

But the lady who spelled Barry for me was nice to do that. Even if I do know how to spell it. Which I do because I have a cousin Barry and he is so cute and he knows everything about computers and he is my favorite, but he is only twelve still so he is my baby cousin, because I am older after today.

No. I am older already today. Today I am thirteen. Which is Teen Age. So now I can do things like Beauty, Mim, and Faithful. But Autumn can't do things yet like run away because she's only eleven.

I sat down in the South Street Market at a little round table and someone had left two napkins and a white paper bag. I folded the paper bag neatly. That is one of my best things, next to jokes and telling where streets are. I fold so neatly. I fold laundry for Mama. She can't fold neatly. And I put the napkins on top of the bag and if someone came and said it was theirs, I would give it to them. But nobody did.

The table was across from a bakery with a big window where three men were making bread and rolls and I watched them and I had thinking that I would tell Mim my sister and she would say That is so interesting, Fancy.

People walked by me with packages and they had babies in strollers and they had babies on their chest and one mama had her baby on her shoulders. I said, That is a cute cute baby. And the mama smiled at me and said thank you. Why did she thank me? I don't know.

I wish I had a baby. Mim my sister says I am too young. I know that. I know I'm special, but I'm not a dope! Mim says having a baby is not a good idea for me. But I think it's a good idea. I think this is my pretty good mind having pretty good thinking thoughts. Because I like babies. I could take very good care of a baby. Never leave it alone. Never. And feed it all the time. And someday I will. But not now. I know that.

People in the South Street Market were eating things and I wished I had packed a sandwich and chocolate cookies like a picnic, which we have sometimes when we visit my twin baby sisters in the cemetery, and I was hungry and everything of food looked so good. I love oranges and a skinny man was eating an orange at the table next to me. And I love cookies and a boy skated by and he was eating from a bag of chocolate cookies.

I hit my head with both hands, which Mrs. Sokolow my teacher I love doesn't allow, which is a poem, but I was not in her class, so I hit my head three times because I am *so stupid* for not taking my money from my Abraham Lincoln the great president bank, which I could have bought something with.

So then. So then I had to think about something else. Which was how funny things are in my family, which is why I like my family. For instance, which is something Mim my sister says, for instance, there's a joke I like and I can tell it to everybody and make them laugh. Knock knock. Who's there? Sez. Sez who? Sez you! and that is my special favorite joke. I have liked that joke since I was very small and young. Sez you! It can make me laugh anytime. Sez you! And I can make my sisters laugh, too.

I'll tell you something else funny I did when I was little. I went to school without underpants. Ha ha ha! But I didn't wear a skirt. I wore pants and I was so silly I thought I had enough pants on and now every day Mim my sister says Are you wearing underpants, Fancy, quote unquote, which is something she taught me when you say something that somebody else says, and it looks like this "" like little fingernails in the air talking to each other. Mama says I love my coffee, coffee and me, quote unquote.

I drink coffee, but not Autumn my sister, too young, which I'm glad of because sometimes she is mean and says I am a hog of attention quote unquote and I don't want her to have nice things like coffee if she's saying mean things. Mim my sister never says mean things and she taught me parens for my special writing in school, which are these ( ) and it looks like two people going to kiss, ha ha! It is a very good funny word, almost like parents, but it isn't. Mim says use parens when you want to write something extra.

Okay! Extra! Parens! I love lemon pie more than chocolate cookies or oranges or coffee. Parens. And that is one thing that made me mad about myself for running away because Mama always makes lemon pie on my birthday and I was having thinking that everybody else was eating my lemon pie. So I was mad. And then I was sad.

After I sat in the South Street Market for a long time thinking about lemon pie, and looking at all the babies and people eating food, I got tired of sitting there. So I walked to the door and the guard at the door said Hello, young lady, and I said Hello, young man, and he laughed and he said Have a good day, and I said I am having a pretty good day because it's my birthday and I ran away, but I ran away too soon before the lemon pie.

You ran away, he said, and he laughed some more like it was one of my jokes and he took my arm and he said If you ran away I have to tell the police.

So I got scared because I don't want police because once they came to our house and my dad was crying because somebody wanted money he owed which made everyone sad and crying in our house because he didn't have the money, and I hate it. I HATE it when people cry. I don't like crying. Period. Quote unquote. Parens. Period. PERIOD.

So I said let go of my arm and I didn't say please and I didn't say it with my polite voice like Mama says I have to, especially you she says quote unquote which she explained to me means because I am special and some people are dumb quote unquote and don't know me and think I am bad or something, so I always have to be polite but that is hard.

Why? Just because! That's what I say. Just because and I like that song that goes Because because because because, and there's more words but those are my favorite words and I sing them and cover my ears if someone asks me too many questions.

So I went outside the door and it was raining on the street, and the guard man was looking at me through the window and I walked away very fast and I wanted to laugh so I wouldn't be scared. I went to the corner and I was laughing very hard and I saw this boy who was cute, I liked him, and I wanted to tell him that funny thing I did when I went to school without underpants so he would laugh too and then he would like me.

He was leaning on the mailbox on the corner and I went up to him and said, Do you want to hear a funny story? He made me a bad face and said, Get lost, stupid. So I didn't tell him my joke about underpants. Too bad for him.

Beauty my sister says she will get married to a boy someday when she's ready. I want to get married, too. Mim my sister says she will go to New York City and she will NOT get married and I can visit her there. I wished I could see her right then because it was raining a lot and I was getting wet and she would tell me what to do.

I was trying to have good thinking about what to do, but it was raining too hard to make my brains work, so I went back to the South Street Market and the guard man said Hello, baby, and I said I am not the baby of my family, that is Autumn my sister and he said Oh, is that so. And I said Yes, it is so, you can ask Mim my sister or my dad, they will tell you. And then he didn't answer me, he made that shrug with his shoulders and he walked away into a room, and I went back to my table with the paper bag and the napkin and it was still across from the bakery with men making bread in the big window.

But someone else was sitting at the next table, not the skinny man with the orange. A lady and a boy. The lady was talking on her cell phone. The boy was reading a book and I saw the word underpants on the cover. I can read that word I said. He didn't answer. I reached over and said Hello, excuse me, I'm talking to you. I can read that word underpants. I bet you didn't know I could read that word.

The boy looked at me and said Retard and went back to reading his book. The lady said in her cell phone Wait a second, Jan, and she put it down and slapped the boy and said Don't talk to the nice girl that way. Then she smiled at me but I was sorry for the boy because he looked like he wanted to cry, and I don't like slapping and I hate crying, so I got up and walked away.

And I had thoughts to myself that this was like running away again because I was running away from that table and a lady who slaps and that made THREE times this morning I ran away. So it was a lot, and I found another table and sat down. And guess what? Another lady in a red and green coat and a hat with red and yellow and green stripes and a big green tassel sat down with me and said What's a big girl like you doing sucking your thumb?

I looked down and she was right I was sucking my thumb IN PUBLIC which Beauty my sister told me is a bad thing. I pulled out my thumb and I said Autumn my sister sucks her thumb too. When she is not being mean we do it together.

Why do you do that? the lady said and she leaned close to me and the tassel on her hat was shaking. You're too big to suck your thumb she said.

We like to do it I said and it tastes good.

The lady made a face at me. Tastes good she said. I'll tell you what tastes good. Ice cream tastes good. You want some ice cream?

Yes I said.

Well I'll get you some if you promise to stop sucking your thumb.

I had thoughts about this and I wanted that ice cream especially if she would get me bubble gum pink which is my favorite, but what if I had to stop sucking at night and all the time? That gave me bad thoughts. Then I remembered I should not take money or food from anyone but my family and she was still looking at me so I said Nooooo, I don't want ice cream, and she said Are you sure? And I said Nooo, I don't want ice cream, which made two times I said that lie.

And that's when I cried because lying means I'm a bad girl. Now what, the lady said, and I told her That is a lie about ice cream and I ran away today.

Then she looked at me with a big surprised face like there was a window in her head and she just opened it, and she said Ran away! Why did you do that?

I told her about my twin baby sisters and Mama crying.

Ohhh she said is that right? And she petted my head and said You should go home, honey, everyone is worrying about you. Do you want me to walk you home and I said Okay, and so she did but she was halfway nice and halfway mean. She chased me just because I wanted to look at things like the cute little dogs in a pet store window and a funny plant with red flowers hanging down and some other stuff, but she wouldn't let me stop or anything. She yelled Go on, keep walking, don't stop, your mother is worrying. And she said more things like Git, go on, girl, go on, I'm not leaving until you're home. And at the corner of Madison Street which has a lot of cars and trucks she yelled at me really loud to WATCH OUT, but I know how to be careful crossing and I am slow, but I am not dumb. And I said so but she grabbed my arm and she yanked me so I didn't like her and I was glad I didn't let her buy me ice cream. And once when her striped hat with the big tassel fell off I didn't even pick it up for her. So there, too.

We came to my house and she knocked on the door and she said to Mim my sister, I think I have someone here that you're looking for.

And Mim yelled, Mama, everybody, here's Fancy!

And my mama came running to the door and she was crying! So I said, It's my birthday! No crying on my birthday or I have to run away again. And I stamped my foot just like Faithful my sister when she has a temper. And I yelled Good-bye!

And I was going to go down the porch stairs, but all my sisters started talking and pulling me into the house and saying things like Mama's happy you're home, we were worried, where were you, why did you run away, what did you do, and so many questions I put my hands over my ears and shouted Because because because about ten times. Then they all grabbed me and my mind said Uh-oh! they're going to be mad at you for yelling, Fancy!

But I was wrong.

Wrong wrong wrong wrong.

They hugged and kissed and wrapped me all up in their arms like I was my own birthday present!

And they put ribbons in my hair and stuck stars

on my face but Mama was crying again and even though she said it was happy tears because I was home I didn't like it.

So I said I am going to tell a joke and make everyone laugh. I am going to make you laugh, Mama.

So then I told my knock knock joke and all my sisters and Mama too yelled SEZ YOU at the end.

And we all laughed and laughed and laughed.

Then we went into the kitchen and ate lemon pie.

And that was my best birthday ever.

Opposite of Miffy

by Lisa Yee

It all comes from not knowing how to reverse. If I had just reversed properly I would never have seen the inside of a police station, been forced to babysit, or consumed raw fish.

My name is Casey Walden and I am a teenager. Well, if I can make it to tomorrow then I will be a teenager, but the odds are against me. It's been a rough five weeks. Here's what happened and this is the truth, the whole truth, and nothing but the truth. . . .

My brother, Bruce, and I needed to go to One Buck Bargains. I was looking for glitter gel pens and he wanted another toilet plunger for the dumb sculpture he's building in the backyard. Bruce just got his license and to hear him talk you'd swear he was

Speed Racer. Yet, when he's behind the wheel, Bruce hunches over and drives like an old granny.

By the time we made it to One Buck Bargains, I was feeling pretty antsy when Bruce spied one of those electric carts. You know, the ones for people who have trouble walking.

"Hey, Casey, I dare you to take it for a spin!"

Naturally, I said no. But that didn't stop Bruce from hopping in and zipping down the aisles. I had to admit it did look like fun.

"You're chicken, aren't you?" Bruce slowed down to examine a bag of feathers, tossed them into the basket, and sped up again.

"I am not," I said, as I tried to keep up with him.

"You are too," he insisted. "Cluck, cluck, cluck...."

Oooooh, he made me so angry! Bruce has been calling me a chicken ever since I refused to go on Monstroso the Roller Coaster of Death two years ago.

"Cluck, cluck...."

"Oh, all right!" I growled, shoving him out of the electric cart and settling in.

"Hey, dork, you have to put it in reverse." Bruce smirked.

"I know that," I lied. It was my first time driving, unless you counted the mini-putt-putt car I had when I was little. However, that vehicle was powered by my feet running along the sidewalk.

Finally, I squeezed the lever on the handle and all of a sudden I was going backward. Wheeee! See, it wasn't so hard. Only, the cart kept backing up, *beep, beep, beep,* and I couldn't get it to stop! *Beep, beep, beep* . . . where were the brakes? How do I use the brakes? *Beep, beep, beep. . . .*

As it turns out I didn't even need the brakes. I used a display of Wispy Waffle Wafers instead.

CRASH!!!! CRUNCH!!!

Wispy Waffle Wafers everywhere! Crushed Wispy Waffle Wafers.

"What did you do that for?" Bruce shouted before disappearing down the detergent aisle.

"You there! Young lady, freeze!"

I looked up to see a One Buck Bargain man barreling toward me. "I just put up that display," he sputtered. "It's one hundred and fifty packages of Wispy Waffle Wafers!" He got on his knees and picked up a package. "They're all broken. I can't sell these now. Do you have any idea what this costs?"

"One hundred and fifty bucks?" I answered meekly.

"That's it!" he yelped. "A juvenile delinquent *and* a comedian? There's only one place for a kid like you!"

Where was Bruce? What would my parents say? Would I die in prison?

When the police finally arrived, I extended my arms to be handcuffed.

"That's not necessary," Officer Graham assured me. She was nothing like those scary cops on television. In fact, she looked like my Aunt Sally, except that Aunt Sally never carries a lethal weapon.

My parents were waiting at the police station when we arrived. Mom was trying to act calm, but I could tell she was freaking out by the way she gripped her purse. Dad was trying to look in control. I was trying not to cry.

The only thing I knew for sure was that I was going to need to update my list of the Top Five Worst Experiences of My Life. Other Top Fivers included Miles Dunn farting loudly in science class and blaming it on me, and the time I wore a clown costume to school for dress-up day—and got the date wrong.

"She's only twelve," my father pleaded. "Casey's a smart kid. She just did something incredibly stupid."

After what seemed like forever, Officer Graham called me over. "Casey, you're getting a second chance. The malicious mischief charges have been dropped," she said.

For the first time since backing up I was able to breathe normally.

When we got home Bruce was already in bed, faking sleep . . . at 7 PM on a Saturday, that coward! He did nothing to defend me. But if I had imagined my bad dream was over, I was wrong. It had only just begun.

The letter of apology I could understand, but what about the rest of the punishment? "You're kidding!" I gasped.

"This is no joke," my father assured me.

"But Bruce dared me. . . ."

"This is not about Bruce," my mother said.

"No fair!" I wailed.

Grounded? Babysit? EVERY DAY after school? Suddenly, prison was looking like an attractive alternative. Dad had paid for the damages and I now owed $150, plus sales tax, to cover the Wispy Waffle Wafers. Unless I wanted to rob a bank (no, thank you), babysitting was my only way out of debt. Officer Graham knew someone at the police station who had a neighbor who knew someone who was in desperate need of a sitter.

"Why does this have to happen to me?" I protested.

"Why did the chicken cross the road?" Bruce asked.

The next day, directly after school, I trudged toward my punishment and rang the bell. When the door finally opened my jaw dropped.

"What are YOU doing here?" Miffy asked.

"What are YOU doing here?" I answered.

"I live here," she said, looking me up and down. I hate it when people do that.

Okay, so maybe I am not the most fashionable person on the planet. I dress for comfort. At least my clothes are always clean, except for that one week when my mom went on strike from doing laundry.

"I'm here to babysit your little sister," I clued her in.

"I don't have a little sister," sniffed Miffy. "Go away. Shoo!"

I handed her the address from Officer Graham.

"Well, you've probably messed up," Miffy said. "Aren't you that girl who wore a clown costume to school?"

Miffy Vanderloo inhabited a perpetual state of stuck-up-ness. Clear skin, beautiful hair, and lots of money left her with an air of entitlement that she wore well. We could have been in a fashion magazine together. Only, I'd be the "before" and she would be the "after."

Just as I was about to bolt, Miffy's mother appeared. "You must be Casey!" she gushed, dragging me inside. "Come in, come in!"

The house was gorgeous and so was Ms. Vanderloo. She was a grown-up version of Miffy, all shiny and bright.

"Mother, what is going on?" Miffy whined.

At least that was one thing we had in common. Miffy and I were both confused.

"This is Casey," her mother informed her. "She is going to be your babysitter until Nanny Pat gets back from Hawaii in six weeks."

"NOOOOOOOO!!!" Miffy and I cried at the same time.

Ms. Vanderloo looked me up and down. "How old are you, Casey?"

"Almost thirteen," I told her. "I have a birthday coming up soon."

"Hmmm . . . I thought you'd be at least sixteen since I was told you were in a driving accident. Oh, well, at least you are still older than Miffy. She's eleven. I suppose it will be all right. I just don't like the idea of my Miffy home alone. Well, have to run. Have fun, girls!"

As if serving time with Miffy weren't torture enough, Bruce continued to be a jerk. The words "cluck, cluck, cluck," had taken on a new and more dramatic meaning. But worse, he still wouldn't even admit that he was involved in the accident.

One night, during week three, Ms. Vanderloo was working late again so she left dinner in the refrigerator. I was bummed because Mom was making her famous Tuna Taco Casserole.

"That's dinner???" I squealed.

"Yesss," Miffy answered, as if I were asking a trick question.

I had never tried sushi and had no intention of eating raw fish anytime soon.

"Try it, it's good," Miffy urged. She expertly plucked a piece with her chopsticks, dipped it in soy sauce, and devoured the whole thing in one barbaric bite.

"No, thanks, I'm not hungry."

"What's the matter?" Miffy smirked. "Are you chicken?"

Oooooooooh, those are fighting words! I grabbed a pair of chopsticks, plunged them into the safest thing I could find on the plate, a small lump of green mashed potatoes, and popped it into my mouth.

I was still reeling by the time my nostrils had cleared out and my eyeballs were back in my head. Gagging and wheezing, I managed to croak, "What was that???"

"Wasabi," Miffy said, laughing. "You're just supposed to put a little of it on your sushi! Here, quick, eat this!"

I didn't know if I should trust her, but since I was dying, what did I have to lose? The ginger did help, I must admit. I was so grateful I even let Miffy talk me into taking a bite of sushi. Though it was far from fantastic, I survived.

The next day I brought a surprise for Miffy.

"What is that?" From the look on her face you would have thought I had handed her a dead squirrel in a pie pan.

"Tuna Taco Casserole," I explained. "Try it."

"Noooooo. . . ."

"Hey," I reminded her. "I tried sushi."

Miffy took a nibble, then another, eating her way through both my serving and hers. After that, we were friends. Well, okay, truthfully? We were never friends, but we weren't enemies anymore.

One afternoon Miffy and I were sharing a bowl of popcorn and watching *Oprah*.

"Today's topic is appreciating your family," Oprah told us.

"Bor-ing," Miffy said, faking a yawn.

"Do you appreciate your mom?" I asked.

"Well," Miffy said, looking about as deep as she could get without standing in a hole. "I appreciate her credit cards."

"Don't you get along?"

As Oprah consoled a woman, Miffy put down the popcorn bowl. "It's hard to say, since we never talk." For a moment she looked sort of sad, but quickly perked up. "But what does it matter, as long as I get my way? Besides, Nanny Pat talks to me all the time. In fact, sometimes I can't get her to shut up."

Suddenly, Miffy's big house full of expensive things seemed very empty. I couldn't wait to get home to my family.

As the Miffy days dragged by, at least I had my birthday to look forward to. My parents always throw me a big party and this year I was certain it was going to be the best one ever. Thirteen years old, a teenager at last!!! I planned to have a BBQ with a Surf's Up theme and. . . .

"Excuse me? That's funny, I thought you said no birthday party." I laughed.

"Casey," my father said, sounding uncomfortable, "grounded means grounded. No party. Sorry, honey."

"Sweetheart," my mother added, "this hurts us more than it hurts you."

"Yes," my father agreed. "But it's for your own good."

"When you're older, you'll thank us for this," Mom assured me.

"Don't count your party chickens before they hatch," Bruce chirped up from the couch.

"Ohmygosh, they're not even going to give you a party?" Miffy was dumbstruck. I was mesmerized by how she could French-braid her own hair without even looking in a mirror. "That's, like, insane," Miffy continued. "They owe you a party. I'm pretty sure it's a law. Do you want me to call my mom's lawyer? He can convince anyone of anything."

"It's okay, really."

"No, it's not okay. If my mom ever said I couldn't have a party, I'd stop speaking to her. Or, I know, I'd threaten to go live with my dad. Whenever I do that, Mom gives me whatever I want. Like last year I wanted to hire a limo for my birthday and my mother refused. But all I had to do was say, 'Daddy will get me one,' and she totally caved in! It was so easy. I had the best birthday. You probably heard about it. Everyone at school was sooooo jealous of me!"

In fact, I had heard of it. Miffy's parties were events, whereas mine would be nonexistent.

"You should freeze your parents out," Miffy suggested. "It always works for me."

"I'm okay without a party," I tried to explain to Miffy. "I think my parents are trying to teach me some sort of lesson."

"Can't they teach you after the party's over?"

"The party is over," I sighed.

I stared at Miffy as she went on and on about how mean my parents were. In social science we were studying other societies, but afternoons with Miffy were like an advanced college course. She was a whole society unto herself. Miffy was so self-absorbed I half expected her to disappear at any moment. If I were to ever evolve as a human being, I would need to be the opposite of Miffy.

Today is my thirteenth birthday. I am officially a teenager.

It seems like it's taking forever for my parents and Bruce to get home. Where are they? I've been sitting on the front porch for over an hour.

At last they arrive. As we walk into the house, classical music greets us. Mom drops her bags when she reaches the dining room. On the table is a big cake decorated in red rosettes reading "13 Wonderful Years!" Balloons and streamers hang from the ceiling.

My father turns to my mother. "I thought we agreed, no party for Casey this year!"

Mom is speechless. Finally she sputters, "I didn't do this, did you?"

Dad shakes his head and then they both turn to Bruce. "Did you do this?"

"Hello?" he says. "Do I look crazy?"

"Well, then, who did?" my father asks.

"Look," I point to a card propped up against the cake. "There's something addressed to the two of you."

Mom tears open the envelope. She takes a sharp breath as she reads the card and then hands it to Dad. A funny look crosses his face.

"What?" Bruce asks, annoyed.

"Read this," Dad instructs him.

To Mom and Dad,
It's been a wonderful 13 years.
Today's not just my birthday,
but a celebration of all the years
I have had you for parents. Thank you.
Love always,
Casey

Bruce puts down the card. "I don't get it."

"Casey is throwing *us* a birthday party," Mom explains, dabbing her eyes with a napkin.

I'm afraid my mother's going to start bawling so I shout, "Hey, let's get this party started!"

My parents are giddy as they open their presents. I can't stop grinning. Mom pretends to swoon as she clutches her coupon, good for two weeks' worth of laundry. Dad can't stop laughing at the cartoon I drew of me in a jail made of Wispy Waffle Wafers.

"Casey," Mom asks, as I serve her a second slice of chocolate cake, "if you're grounded, how did you manage to get the cake and all the decorations?"

"That's right," my father asks between bites. "You know you're only allowed to go directly to Miffy's house and back."

Bruce has been unusually quiet, but he looks up to hear my answer.

"I had help," I say, putting on my mystery-girl look. "But I'm sworn to secrecy."

The rest of the afternoon we play charades, my Dad's favorite game, and then pore over family photo albums. Everyone, even Bruce, has a great time.

After cleaning the dining room and washing the dishes, I wander into the backyard. Bruce is working on his sculpture. I hand him some feathers and he attaches them to a hubcap.

"Hey, Bruce, I owe you one."

"You owe me more than one," he says. "You owe me twenty bucks for getting the cake and stuff."

"I'll pay you back, right after I finish paying Dad the money I owe him," I promise.

"You know," Bruce muses, "I do feel sorta bad for daring you to drive the cart. I never expected you to reverse like that, though the look on your face when you crashed was priceless! I'd even say it was worth twenty dollars, if you know what I mean!"

Huh?

"Look, Casey." Bruce faces me. "You don't owe me anything. Consider it a birthday present. Let's just forget that any of this ever happened. Hand me some more feathers, will you?"

Maybe Bruce could forget, but I knew I never would.

I will always remember my thirteenth birthday as the year my parents bailed me out of jail, and the weeks spent babysitting the selfish Miffy Vanderloo, and the day my brother and I became friends. It was also when I discovered that giving a birthday party can be even better than getting one.

The Girl in the Mirror

by Cynthia D. Grant

Was she pretty or ugly? She couldn't decide. She was thirteen years old today—thirteen!—and stuff she'd always believed, she didn't believe anymore; and stuff she'd never thought about before crowded into her mind, even when she tried to push it out.

For example, her dad. She'd always been so proud of him. Even last spring, coaching her basketball team. Joking with the girls, making them all laugh. Now she wondered: Did they *really* think he was funny? Or was he so unfunny they felt sorry for him, and laughed to be nice? She wasn't sure. The other day when Steffi and Barrett were at the house, and he'd said, what had he said, something about boys and they'd laughed (being polite?), she had cringed all over. *Dad, please shut up!* She'd wanted to scream it.

Megan studied her nose in the bathroom mirror. Two dark tunnels plowed into her head. Nostrils. What a word. Why did she have to have nostrils? *May I offer you a nostril? No, thanks; I've got two*. And her mouth. She looked like one of those, what do you call them, marionettes, when she smiled. Quit smiling! When she smiled, people could see her braces. They looked like tiny straitjackets all over her teeth.

Straitjackets! Was she going insane without knowing it? If she *was* going insane, would Steffi tell her? Probably not; she was too nice. When she'd said, "Tell me the truth, Steff. Is my nose really awful?" Steffi said, "No, it's fine." Which it obviously wasn't.

Let's face it: She should probably wear a bag over her head.

A bag! She shrank with embarrassment at the memory. She had tried to explain nicely to Dad that she didn't want to hurt his feelings—but could he please, *please*, not park his old VW in front of the school? It was yellow. *Bright* yellow. It looked like clowns should climb out of it, or some geek delivering pizza. On top of that, he insisted on kissing her good-bye: *Have a good day, honey!* How? He'd just ruined it. And number three, he'd grown that stupid beard that made him look like a hippie. Pathetic!

Dad hadn't seemed upset; he said he understood. But later, when he'd picked her up at Steffi's, he drove up *wearing a grocery bag over his head*, complete with sunglasses over the eye holes. She almost died when she saw him.

"I know you don't want people to see me," he said.

Steffi and her mom both laughed—but what were they really thinking? Imagine if he'd been stopped by a cop. It would've been so awful. It *was* so awful. But she had to keep that stupid smile on her face— "Bye, Steff! See you tomorrow!"—like she thought it was funny, too, when the truth was she practically had to hold up the corners of her mouth with both hands. She felt like sobbing. Or opening a trapdoor beneath the driver's seat.

Dad look shocked and ashamed when he saw that she was crying. "Come on, honey," he said. "Where's your famous sense of humor?"

Gone. Just gone, and she didn't know where, like her dolls and her princess costume.

Her mother knocked lightly on the bathroom door. "Hurry up, honey. We have a reservation."

"I can't go," Meg said. "I have to study."

"On a Friday night? For what?"

"A test."

"What kind of test?"

A lie detector test! she wanted to scream. Why couldn't they just leave her alone? They acted like her birthday was a big fat deal. They wanted to take her out for pizza and a movie, to celebrate. Celebrate what? That she didn't have any friends? That she would probably be voted *Most Likely To Spend the Rest of Her Life with Her Parents*? What if she ran into Steffi, or the others? Why didn't her friends like her anymore? Was it something she'd done? Could someone please tell her what? Why had all of them—Nicole, Barrett, Jessica, Katie, even Steffi—turned against her?

It was so obvious all last week. Whenever she walked up to join them, they quit talking or changed the subject. She'd caught a fragment of conversation: They were going somewhere. To a slumber party? Bowling? Wherever they were going, she wasn't invited, and they didn't want to hurt her feelings.

Think again!

And once, when she headed back to class after lunch, she heard them laughing as she walked away. Laughing at her. Behind her back. Even Steffi! How could they be so *mean*? She was never that mean. Well, sometimes she was, when she was in a bad mood. But usually only to her parents.

The girl in the mirror morphed like Silly Putty.

How many times had she stared at herself like this? A million? A zillion? Sometimes she thought: *Oh, wow. I'm pretty.* Other times she thought she looked so awful she was ashamed to go out in public. And don't look in the magnifying mirror. Big mistake! Look at all that hair on her upper lip! Was she supposed to be a man? Did all the other girls have invisible mustaches? Did Steffi have holes all over her face? What was the point of pores? Her face looked like the tennis court at school before it was repaved. She should go to a whatchamacallit, a skin doctor. But when she'd suggested it, her mom, who used to be so sweet and understanding, but now was always being picky, or thought she was a comedian (she wasn't), said: "Everybody has pores, honey. There's nothing wrong with your skin. You have a beautiful complexion."

Of course she had to say that! She's my mother! What would you call this thing on my chin? If it gets any bigger, people will think it's my *head*. They'll be talking to my pimple: *So, Megan, what's up?* Megan! It was the perfect name for a dog. A big, floppy Lab or a golden retriever. *Here, Meggy. Good girl. Now, give me your paw....*

Kids, not parents, should get to choose their own names.

Kids should get to choose—no offense—their own parents.

She wasn't even sure—it made her feel so bad to think this—she loved her parents anymore. She used to love bananas. Now they made her throw up. How could she be sure that what she felt for them was love? When they were mad at her, they said they loved her just as much. Sometimes she felt like—she hated to say it—she hated them. Last weekend, when Mom said she couldn't go to the mall—"You're going to stay here until you finish all your homework"— Meg would've pushed the eject button, if she could've found one; sending her mother through the roof and into outer space, trailing instructions: *I want you to write Aunt Diane a thank-you letter. Then do the dishes. Then mow the lawn. Then rake the leaves—*

Why was she the one who always had to do *every-thing*, while they sat around and read the paper? She wasn't their slave! They should've had another kid to boss around. Her dad said, "We did. But we were so mean to her she ran away."

Was that supposed to be *funny*? It wasn't! Most of her friends had brothers and sisters. They couldn't stand each other but that wasn't the point. Didn't her parents like children? And why did they have to be so *old*? A new girl at school saw her dad and asked,

"Is that your grampa?" Much to her amazement, Meg heard herself say, "Yes." Couldn't her father grow hair on top of his head, instead of out of his ears? Couldn't her mother wear a little makeup?

And what was the point of writing thank-you letters? She'd already thanked Aunt Diane on the phone. Besides, why did she have to thank her for pajamas with kitties and puppies all over them? She was turning thirteen today. Not three. Luckily, the pajamas arrived in the mail, so Aunt Diane hadn't seen her face when she'd opened the package, which looked just like the time in the school cafeteria when she'd found a used Band-Aid in her sloppy joe. Mom said it was the thought that counted. Okay, so, next time send a card, not a present. But she would never say that. She loved Aunt Diane.

Didn't she? How could she be sure what love felt like? Was this the way everyone felt? She loved ice cream, too. *So why don't you marry it?* That idiot Dustin said such stupid stuff! Like today, at lunch, in the school cafeteria. He'd pointed at that thing on her chin, and said, "What's that?" What did he *think* it was? Dutch Elm disease? Everybody heard his foghorn voice. He might as well have announced it over the P.A. system! So what if they were friends in kindergarten? He had a mustache that looked like chocolate milk. It probably *was* chocolate milk. Could people see *her* mustache and—she'd never noticed un-til now—the colorless hair all over her cheeks? Her face looked like a giant *peach*. Was that what people were saying behind her back? *Don't look now but here comes Peach Head*.

Her father tapped on the bathroom door. "Other people have to get in there, too."

"Use the backyard."

"Sorry, I didn't hear you, honey."

"Nothing."

Did her friends really like her or didn't they? Some days it seemed like they did. But the other day, when she wore that brown sweater Granny made (she knew that was a mistake but her mother insisted), everybody was like: *Oh, hi, Meg*—but acting funny, like they couldn't wait for her to walk away so they could say stuff. *Did you see that sweater? Her mom knitted it out of her dad's beard*.

Why did her friends seem so different? Had she done something really dumb? When Barrett sang the song she planned to do in the talent show, and asked her what she thought, why had she answered, "Well, it's a little . . . long"? Everybody else thought it sounded fine! Was that why they'd changed? Or was she the one who'd changed? She wanted to feel the same way she'd always felt. Was that what turning thirteen meant: that you outgrew happiness like a pair of old shoes? Plaid sneakers! What had her mother been thinking? "Look what I found for you at the yard sale, Meggy. Aren't they darling? And they're brand-new."

Of course they were new! Even Granny wouldn't have worn them. She hadn't even shown those awful sneakers to Steffi and they'd been best friends forever. Why didn't Steffi want to be friends anymore? Was it the brown sweater?

All morning she had waited for Steffi to say something. Finally, at their lockers, which were right next to each other, she'd said, "Hey, guess what, Steff! It's my birthday today."

Steffi got this guilty look on her face. "Sorry," she said. "I guess I forgot."

Megan felt herself turn burning red. Every drop of blood in her entire body was stuffed inside her head.

All she said was, "That's okay."

She waited, in case Steffi said something else. The silence stretched between them like a thread of bubble gum.

"Well," Meg said, "I'd better get to class." And she walked down the hall, Steffi's eyes on her back; her arms and legs were as stiff as if they belonged to someone else, as if they'd come from the Lost and Found table.

What had she expected? Crepe paper and balloons? A parade and a shower of confetti? She was thirteen, not three. She wasn't a baby anymore. Now, when she fell down during a basketball game and practically killed herself, she couldn't cry. She had to pretend it didn't hurt. The party was over.

It was funny: When she was little, she couldn't *wait* to be a teenager!

About as funny as her father's jokes.

She was tired of pretending to be grown up. She was tired of pretending she wasn't pretending. She'd transfer to a different school, where nobody knew her. People would be nicer. She'd be nicer, too. No matter how badly one of her teammates blew it during a game, she wouldn't get mad or call her an idiot. After all, it was supposed to be fun. If only her mother wouldn't come to every game. Meg could hear her, above the crowd, yelling: *Good try, Meggy!* like she was four years old and learning to tie her shoes.

If only her parents didn't care about her so much!

That was crazy. Everybody knew it was great to have parents like hers. She was so lucky! So why did they *annoy* her so much? She acted like the cat lately. Her parents petted her and loved her and she tolerated it, tail twitching, until she couldn't stand it anymore, and bit them.

She couldn't figure it out. Who *was* she? Her skin felt too tight. Her legs were too long. One side of her hair flipped up; the other, under. Her feet were too big. Even her eyebrows looked strange. But hadn't Natalie said Becky said Richie told her that Bobby Franzini thought she was cute? Could that be true? He was such a nice guy. She'd always liked him. Or had Natalie said that just to make fun of her?

Bobby probably said it because he felt sorry for her. *Poor Megan. Look at that sweater. She's such a loser.* Her mom and dad always told her she was beautiful. On the inside, too, where it really counted. What good did being beautiful on the *inside* do? Of *course* she knew looks shouldn't be so important! Everybody knew that! But nobody believed it! Did magazines offer 101 tips to improve your inner beauty? It was all about appearances. Was that her fault? When she was little, she looked in the mirror only to wash her face or brush her teeth. Now she couldn't stop looking—and she couldn't bear to look.

Her mom knocked on the bathroom door. "Honey, we've got to go now or we'll miss our reservation. Why don't you wear your new sweater?"

As if she didn't have *enough* problems. What kind of color was *brown*?

On her way through the kitchen she checked the phone machine. The red light wasn't blinking. There were no messages. No one had asked her to come over, or to hang out, or do anything. Her mother always said, *You can invite people, too.*

But what if you asked them and they said no—not because they were busy, but because it was you?

Her mom's car was in the shop so they took the clown car. Megan slouched in the back seat, hoping no one would see her. What if she wrote a sign and held it up? *These aren't my real parents. I'm being kidnapped.* What if her dad was arrested? Would he have to shave?

The pizza place was packed. Everybody seemed to be laughing. If only she could sit at one of those tables where people were having fun.

"Party of three?" asked the hostess.

You call this a party? A night on the town with my parents? Some fun.

She followed the hostess toward the back of the restaurant. *Left, right, left . . .* She could barely walk. Had anyone noticed? Were people staring?

The hostess smiled at her parents. "We're swamped tonight. I'm going to have to put you in here, if that's okay."

Great. Just great. The waitress will need a map to find us. Put me in the restroom for all I care.

Meg stepped into the dark room. It exploded with noise and light. Cameras flashed and people were screaming, *Happy Birthday, Meggy!*

Everybody was there: Steffi, Barrett, Jessica, Katie, Natalie, all the girls on her basketball team. Richie, Peter, Jacob. Even Dustin. And, smiling in the corner, Bobby Franzini.

The girls hugged her and laughed, and said, *Meggy, were you surprised?*

Happy tears filled her eyes. "You guys!" she cried. "You scared me half to death!"

Oh Happy Day!

by Sharon Robinson

It wasn't until 1947 that black men were allowed to play Major League Baseball. Then the Brooklyn Dodgers picked up a player who would change the history of the sport forever. Number 42 came up from the minors in Montreal. He was a tall, handsome, brown-skinned man with an amazing smile and a powerful swing. He brought an aggressive style to the game, torturing pitchers with his speed and guts as he stole bases and took the ultimate risk by stealing home. He played 151 games that first season, despite threats on his life, players spiking him with metal cleats, and pitchers throwing at his head. He responded to racist name-calling by hitting a double, stealing a base, and making it home. He led the league in stolen bases, sacrifice bunts, was second in runs scored, and was named Outstanding Rookie of the Year. As the season ended, a national poll named him the second-most popular man in America, next to comedian Bob Hope. After his ten years with the Dodgers, he retired but continued to work for equal justice in America. For a lifetime of service he received America's highest awards: the Presidential Medal of Freedom and the Congressional Gold Medal.

Most people called this awesome man Jackie Robinson.

I called him Dad.

My special bond with my father began the moment I was born. He adored me. I worshipped him. And, as if by design, we shared a birthday month!

Growing up, we celebrated our birthdays at home. My mom grilled thick sirloin steaks, and my grandmother baked us our favorite cakes.

My brothers, Jackie and David, liked yellow cake with thick chocolate icing while I preferred white cake with rich buttery icing. If I was lucky my grandmother would pull out her decorating tools from her catering days, and make what could have been a wedding cake!

I attached myself to my grandmother's hip so that

I wouldn't miss a moment of the cake's creation. Of course I had another reason for staying by her side— if I was there, she couldn't get the bowl laced with leftover batter into the sink without me licking it clean first.

Grandma blended the cake ingredients and spooned them into cake pans. I lifted the bowl and spoon out of her hands and scooped the remaining batter into my eager mouth.

After Grandma put the cake pans into the pre-heated oven, she made the icing and I took a little break from kitchen surveillance. But I timed my return perfectly. I'd reach her side in time to lick the beaters. The icing was so sweet I could tolerate only small doses at a time.

The next step was the most interesting. I'd climb on a chair to get a better view. Grandma created a funnel out of cloth, attached a medal decorator tip, filled the cloth with frosting, then squeezed. Slowly a garden of pink roses grew around the edge of the cake and down its sides. It was magic! Grandma purposely left the center of the cake free of flowers so she could write my name!

On January 13th, after birthday dinner, Grandma presented me with my cake. I stared at the flickering candles, knowing I'd already been granted my wish. On this one special day of the year, I was the star in my house.

In our home, birthdays were about family first, then friends. We usually had some sort of party. I liked sleepover parties best.

I would invite between six and eight girlfriends to my parties. Dad's trophy room was designated "sleep central." Our sleeping bags took up most of the floor space. The girls always got a good giggle out of being surrounded by signed baseballs, silver bats, bronzed football cleats, and walls crowded with awards and plaques.

The trophy room was located on the lower level of the house. It was strategically placed between the playroom and a family room. Jackie's pool table, the soda fountain, and Dad's indoor golf putting green filled the playroom. My brother forbade me and my friends from touching his pool table for fear we'd scratch the felt surface. We could care less. The soda fountain held a bigger attraction. We took turns making milk shakes and ice-cream sodas and serving them to the girls sitting across the counter on high stools.

After we had our fill of ice cream, we'd flop on the sofa in the family room and take turns performing. There was a floor-to-ceiling stone fireplace in there, and the hearth made a perfect stage. We specialized in Broadway show tunes and knew the moves and lyrics to all of our favorite musicals.

My thirteenth birthday was difficult. After dinner my mother got a call that changed everything. Mom took my friend Candy away from the group. I thought it was strange. When Candy returned we could tell she'd been crying. Mom sat with us and told us that Candy's mom had died.

The news was so shocking, we fell silent. How could Candy's mother die so young? So suddenly. And on my birthday!

Candy decided to stay at the party. The crisis made us closer, but left me frightened for years. If it could happen to Candy, it could happen to me, too.

My thirteenth birthday was my last all-girl party. After that, I started inviting boys. Motown music was big in those days. We had stacks of 45 records. Candy and I baked brownies, filled bowls with potato chips, and hung up little red lights around the room. Dad policed the area before our friends arrived. He tested the lights, making sure that there were enough so that the room wouldn't be too dark. For the rest of the evening, Dad and Mom positioned themselves upstairs in the living room, so they had a clear view of the front door and knew exactly who came and left their house. Dad also made regular rounds through the family room to make sure that no one danced too close.

There were always six or so girls who traveled from New York City and Long Island to our house in Connecticut, so they always slept over. We'd stay up all night going over all the details from the party.

I have vivid memories of my birthdays, but hardly remember how we celebrated my dad's. All I know for sure is that we spent Dad's birthdays quietly. It was a time to gather as a family. A private time to tell him how much we loved him. A time away from public stares and autograph seekers.

My father's birthday came and went with few visible signs of celebration. This fit Dad's style. He wasn't a partying man.

My father died when he was fifty-three years old. It was the most terrifying moment of my life. It was a loss so hard to accept that I survived by blocking out most of the ceremony that accompanied his funeral. For years after Dad died I struggled with what to do on his birthday. Did you still celebrate a birthday when someone you love has passed on?

That first year I woke up vaguely aware that it was my father's fifty-fourth birthday. My immediate reaction was to call Dad to wish him a happy birthday. Then I remembered that he was dead. But if my father was dead, did he really turn fifty-four? I buried my head in my pillow and cried until my chest hurt.

For years after, I did nothing. I didn't call my mother. I didn't visit Dad's grave and put flowers on his tombstone. I didn't listen to music. We didn't gather as a family. Instead, I stayed in my house remembering time spent with my dad.

One of my most cherished memories is of our father-daughter excursions to New York City, which began not long after my father retired from baseball. I was seven.

Dad worked for Chock full o'Nuts—the Starbucks of the fifties and sixties. His office was in the main headquarters above the Madison Avenue coffee shop. Several times a year he would announce that he was taking me with him to the city. The day began with a brief stop at his office. I'd happily sit upon a stool eating a warm pecan-covered brownie with hot chocolate while Dad went upstairs to his office to check his mail. While I ate and played on the stool, the ladies behind the counter entertained me with stories of my dad's days as a baseball player. It was such fun! Dad wouldn't be gone long. When he returned, we'd go on a shopping spree, have lunch together, and head back home.

We always made this trip in Dad's car. A ride in

Dad's car meant at least one round of Edwin Hawkins singing, "Oh Happy Day." I remember the first time I heard the gospel song. I was all dressed up, excited to have my dad's undivided attention. Somewhere along the way, he slipped in the eight-track and transformed the car into a concert hall. The cheery beat and uplifting lyrics made me feel happy. I'd learned to love music from my mother, but she played mostly classical and jazz. This gospel beat stirred a different kind of emotion. I was hooked. From that day on, "Oh Happy Day" became one of my favorite tunes and I never tired of hearing it blast through the speakers in Dad's car.

While I had wonderful memories from when my father was alive, I still hadn't solved my problem of what to do with Dad's birthday now that he was no longer living. Tired of the dilemma, I finally took action. With Mom's permission, we organized a concert with leading gospel artists from across the country. We chose to have the celebration at the Cathedral of St. John the Divine, a massive stone church in New York City.

I was thrilled and relieved when Reverend Jesse Jackson, who had delivered my father's eulogy, and the Edwin Hawkins Singers, who had made "Oh Happy Day" famous, agreed to join in our birthday tribute.

No obstacles could dampen our spirits. When I was warned that the cathedral was difficult to heat, I declared, "We'll wear coats."

As January 31st approached, the excitement built. I felt courageous, proud, and scared. My family had hosted jazz concerts at our home for years, but this was the first time I was responsible for an event this big!

Concert setup took all day. Performers arrived, unloaded their instruments and equipment, and dressed for the night. Committee members raced around, wrapped in wool, getting prepared for show time. The cathedral doors opened at seven. Family, friends, Jackie Robinson fans, and gospel lovers filled the seats, seemingly unfazed by the chill in the air. As the stage lights came on and the first group burst into song, our spirits and the temperature of the chambers soared.

Midway through the evening, my brother David and I welcomed our guests, thanked Reverend Jackson and the performers, and paid a very public tribute to our amazing father on his birthday. As we stepped back, the lights dimmed again as the Edwin Hawkins Singers belted out the emotional lyrics of "Oh Happy Day." Then, I wept.

"Oh Happy Day! Oh Happy Day!"

Over the years, I've taken back January 31st as a

private day. I no longer feel burdened by sadness because I realize how lucky I was to have known my father's love.

And, by the way, on January 31, 2005, my dad would have turned eighty-six.

Lois Lowry

Born on March 20, 1937, in Honolulu, Hawaii, children's author Lois Lowry has lived all over the world.

Lowry's list of fiction includes over 30 books for young people. Twice the recipient of the Newbery Medal, given each year for the most distinguished contribution to children's literature by an American author, Lowry has also received the Regina Medal, the Dorothy Canfield Fisher Award, the Mark Twain Award, the Boston Globe-Horn Book Award, the Bank Street College Award, the National Jewish Book Award, the Chicago Tribune Book Award, and countless other honors for her work. She was the United States nominee for the 2004 Hans Christian Andersen Medal. Her books have been translated into more than twenty languages, and in 1996 her award-winning classic novel *The Giver*, called in translation *Le Passeur*, was chosen by the children of Belgium and France as their favorite.

She is a mother and grandmother and has worked as a photojournalist as well as a writer of fiction.

Ann Cameron

Born in Wisconsin, Ann Cameron lives in Panaja-chel, Guatemala, near Lake Atitlan, a beautiful mountain lake with three massive volcanoes on its shore. Ann is married to Bill Cherry, who is known in Panajachel as "Don Dulce"—in English that would be "Mr. Sweet"—because he gives candy every day of the year to kids on the street. Ann's birthday is October 21st. She has painful memories of childhood birthdays in Wisconsin at which partygoers gave her a spank for each year of her age and "a pinch to grow an inch." She hopes that's no longer a Wisconsin custom.

Ann is the award-winning author of *The Stories Julian Tells* and other story collections about Julian and his friends; her most recent novel, *Colibrí*, concerns a kidnapped Guatemalan twelve-year-old's struggle to get back to her Mayan family. "One Wing" was inspired by the tenth birthday of Ann and Bill's granddaughter, Jessica.

Alma Flor Ada

I was born in Cuba many years ago, on January 3rd, to a wonderful family who loved to tell stories. Since there were few children nearby, trees and books became my favorite friends. I loved to spend time outdoors by the river, watching birds and fish, frogs and turtles. My hometown had no public library, and although my parents were very generous and bought me as many books as they could, I always wanted more. So I would read the books I had over and over again, until I knew them by heart. Maybe that is what got me started on the road to someday writing my own.

I am delighted to speak two languages, since it has helped me make many friends in my travels to different countries of the world. I wish I spoke many more languages!

In addition to reading books and traveling, I love to spend time outdoors, walking and swimming. I have four children and nine grandchildren, and I have always felt that birthdays are very special occasions.

And, yes, I have always loved piñatas!

Amy Goldman Koss

Here are the books I wrote in the dining room with phones, doorbells, children, animals, and smoke detectors screaming around me: *Where Fish Go in Winter*, *The Trouble with Zinny Weston*, *How I Saved Hannukah*, *The Ashwater Experiment*, *The Girls*, *Stranger in Dadland*, *Smoke Screen*, *Strike Two*, *Gossip Times Three*, *Stolen Words*, and *The Cheat* (not necessarily in that order).

But now I've left the dining room and am writing this from a quiet room of my own. Until a few weeks ago this was a dark, spider-infested corner of the garage. But now, thanks to several hairy men, there are bright yellow walls, a shiny green floor, and a huge window. I've dragged my desk and chair and computer in here, stuck some flowers in a vase, and promoted Sweetie, the dog, from family pet to office manager. Listen. Do you hear children fighting? Banging on the piano? Rollerblading through the living room? NO! Do you think I'll be able to write books in my quiet new office?

We shall see.

P.S. My birthday is January 26th. Gifts welcome!

Nora Raleigh Baskin

Nora Baskin is the author of three middle-grade novels, *What Every Girl (Except Me) Knows*, *Almost Home*, and *Basketball (or Something Like It)*. *The Company of Crazies* will be published in spring 2006.

When Nora is not writing for young adults, she is teaching. For the past several years Nora has been writer-in-residence for various public and private schools. She brings a message of individuality and voice. She believes in finding a dream and never giving it up.

By the way, Nora's birthday is May 18th. And although she kind of likes the number 18 and even the month of May, Nora really did hate her birthday for a very long time, for all of the very same reasons Libby does in the story "Celebration."

Lois Metzger

My birthday is December 22nd—a day that is much too close to several major holidays. So when I was growing up I always received "combination presents"—"Happy Birthday! And Happy Hanukah! And Merry Christmas!" But December 22nd is also the second longest night of the year, and the second shortest day of the year. Meaning that on December 22nd the days are getting longer again, starting now.

Along with many short stories, I've also written three novels—*Barry's Sister* (a Parents Magazine Best Children's Book of the Year); *Ellen's Case* (a New York Public Library Book for the Teenaged); and *Missing Girls*, which was included in *The New York Times Parent's Guide to the Best Books for Children*.

I grew up in Queens, New York City, and now live in Greenwich Village, New York City, with my husband, Tony Hiss, a writer, and my teenaged son, Jacob, and a black-and-white cat.

Rita Williams-Garcia

Rita Williams-Garcia was born in Jamaica, Queens, New York on April 13, 1957. Rita writes: "My older sister and brother took every opportunity to point out that my birthday fell on an unlucky number. Their birth numbers were even numbers, lucky numbers. But I took pride in being born on the 13th. I liked defying the odds on being unlucky."

Author of four award-winning novels, Rita Williams-Garcia continues to break new ground in young people's literature. Known for their realistic portrayal of teens of color, Williams-Garcia's works have been recognized by the Coretta Scott King Award Committee, PEN/Norma Klein, and the American Library National Book Award Committee for Young People's Literature, and she participates in various programs to promote literacy. Her titles include *No Laughter Here*, *Every Time a Rainbow Dies*, *Like Sisters on the Homefront*, *Fast Talk on a Slow Track*, and *Blue Tights*.

Rita Williams-Garcia currently lives in Queens, New York, and is the mother of two daughters.

Norma Fox Mazer

I was born on May 15th in New York City, but grew up in Glens Falls, New York, a small town close to the Adirondack Mountains, where my immigrant grandparents settled a century ago. My mother's mother, who died before I was born, came to me in family stories as a bright, energetic, and beautiful blue-eyed woman who could neither read nor write. I often wonder how astonished she might be to know that not only is her granddaughter a writer, but also her great-granddaughter, my oldest daughter, Anne Mazer.

I have published 30 books, including two collections of short stories and three novels written with my husband, Harry Mazer. *After the Rain* was a Newbery Honor Book, and *A Figure of Speech* was a National Book Award nominee. My new novel, *What I Believe*, will be published this year. Presently I teach in the Vermont College Master of Fine Arts Writing for Children and Young Adults program.

Lisa Yee

The year I turned thirteen, my birthday, August 27th, fell on a Sunday. I begged my parents to let me stay home instead of going to church. Finally, they gave in. Later, I learned my Sunday school teacher had planned a surprise party for me. However, since I was a no-show, they had the party without me!

Growing up in Monterey Park, California, I wanted to be a detective like Nancy Drew, or live in an upside-down house like Mrs. Piggle-Wiggle. But what I really, really wanted to be was an author. Only I never told anyone for fear I'd get laughed at.

After college, I wrote commercials, TV specials, newspaper articles—everything but books. Yet instead of fading, my longing to be an author grew stronger. So when my first novel, *Millicent Min, Girl Genius*, won the Sid Fleischman Humor Award in 2004, it was my dream come true, only better. *Stanford Wong Flunks Big-Time* is my second book. I live in South Pasadena, California, with my two children, husband, and Labradoodle dog. You can visit me at my website, www.lisayee.com.

Cynthia D. Grant

Cynthia Grant survived junior high and lives in the mountains outside Cloverdale, California. Twelve of her novels for children and young adults have been published. Her most recent young adult novel was *The Cannibals*, published in 2002. In 1991, she won the first PEN/Norma Klein award for *Phoenix Rising; or How to Survive Your Life.* She is married to high school counselor and good guy Erik Neel; and has two wonderful sons, Morgan and Forest, who wish she wouldn't call them wonderful in print.

Cynthia adds: "I was born on November 23, 1950, Thanksgiving Day. Millions have given thanks for me ever since—or so my Gram believed. When I was eleven, the big brother of one of my friends said that he had something very important to tell me—but couldn't, until I was sixteen and more mature. I wondered and wondered: What could the secret be? Five years later I asked Bob to tell me the secret I'd waited so long to hear. He said, 'What're you talking about? I was just kidding around.' Thus teaching me one of life's most important lessons: Don't take it too seriously."

Sharon Robinson

Sharon Robinson is the author of a memoir, *Stealing Home*; an anthology, *Jackie's Nine: Jackie Robinson's Values to Live By*; and a photographic biography, *Promises to Keep: How Jackie Robinson Changed America* (an ALA Best Book for Young Adults). In 2006, Ms. Robinson will introduce a fictional character, Elijah J. Breeze II, aka Jumper, in her first novel for children, *Safe at Home*.

Ms. Robinson is also an Educational Consultant to Major League Baseball. In this capacity, she created the national character-based education program Breaking Barriers: In Sports, In Life. She also partners with the American Library Assocation to promote literacy. Prior to joining Major League Baseball, she had a twenty-year career as a nurse-midwife and an educator.

Ms. Robinson was born January 13th. She has one son, Jesse Simms, whose November 25th birthday often falls on Thanksgiving Day. Sharon lives in New York City and in St. Croix, U.S. Virgin Islands.